T0064591

MURDER AND THE FAITH HEALER

Volume 7: Zen and the Art of Investtigation

ANTHONY WOLFF

authorHOUSE®

AuthorHouse™
1663 Liberty Drive
Bloomington, IN 47403
www.authorhouse.com
Phone: 1-800-839-8640

This is a work of fiction. All of the characters, names, incidents, organizations, and dialogue
in this novel are either the products of the author's imagination or are used fictitiously.

Published by AuthorHouse 4/7/2014

ISBN: 978-1-4969-0155-2 (sc)
ISBN: 978-1-4969-0156-9 (e)

PREFACE

WHO ARE THESE DETECTIVES ANYWAY?

"The eye cannot see itself" an old Zen adage informs us. The Private I's in these case files count on the truth of that statement. People may be self-concerned, but they are rarely self-aware.

In courts of law, guilt or innocence often depends upon its presentation. Juries do not - indeed, they may not - investigate any evidence in order to test its veracity. No, they are obliged to evaluate only what they are shown. Private Investigators, on the other hand, are obliged to look beneath surfaces and to prove to their satisfaction - not the court's - whether or not what appears to be true is actually true. The Private I must have a penetrating eye.

Intuition is a spiritual gift and this, no doubt, is why *Wagner & Tilson, Private Investigators* does its work so well.

At first glance the little group of P.I.s who solve these often baffling cases seem different from what we (having become familiar with video Dicks) consider "sleuths." They have no oddball sidekicks. They are not alcoholics. They get along well with cops.

George Wagner is the only one who was trained for the job. He obtained a degree in criminology from Temple University in Philadelphia and did exemplary work as an investigator with the Philadelphia Police. These were his golden years. He skied; he danced; he played tennis; he had a Porsche, a Labrador retriever, and a small sailboat. He got married and had a wife, two toddlers, and a house. He was handsome and well built, and he had great hair.

And then one night, in 1999, he and his partner walked into an ambush. His partner was killed and George was shot in the left knee and in his right shoulder's brachial plexus. The pain resulting from his injuries and the twenty-two surgeries he endured throughout the year that followed, left him addicted to a nearly constant morphine drip. By the time he was admitted to a rehab center in Southern California for treatment of his morphine addiction and for physical therapy, he had lost everything previously mentioned except his house, his handsome face, and his great hair.

His wife, tired of visiting a semi-conscious man, divorced him and married a man who had more than enough money to make child support payments unnecessary and, since he was the jealous type, undesirable. They moved far away, and despite the calls George placed and the money and gifts he sent, they soon tended to regard him as non-existent. His wife did have an orchid collection which she boarded with a plant nursery, paying for the plants' care until he was able to accept them. He gave his brother his car, his tennis racquets, his skis, and his sailboat.

At the age of thirty-four he was officially disabled, his right arm and hand had begun to wither slightly from limited use, a frequent result of a severe injury to that nerve center. His knee, too, was troublesome. He could not hold it in a bent position for an extended period of time; and when the weather was bad or he had been standing for too long, he limped a little.

George gave considerable thought to the "disease" of romantic love and decided that he had acquired an immunity to it. He would never again be vulnerable to its delirium. He did not realize that the gods of love regard such pronouncements as hubris of the worst kind and, as such, never allow it to go unpunished. George learned this lesson while working on the case, *The Monja Blanca*. A sweet girl, half his age and nearly half his weight, would fell him, as he put it, "as young David slew the big dumb Goliath." He understood that while he had no future with her, his future would be filled with her for as long as he had a mind that could think. She had been the victim of the most vicious swindlers he had ever encountered. They had successfully fled the country, but not the range of George's determination to apprehend them. These were master criminals, four of them, and he secretly vowed that he would make them fall, one by one. This was a serious quest. There was nothing quixotic about George Roberts Wagner.

While he was in the hospital receiving treatment for those fateful gunshot wounds, he met Beryl Tilson.

Beryl, a widow whose son Jack was then eleven years old, was working her way through college as a nurse's aid when she tended George. She had met him previously when he delivered a lecture on the curious differences between aggravated assault and attempted murder, a not uninteresting topic. During the year she tended him, they became friendly enough for him to communicate with her during the year he was in rehab. When he returned to Philadelphia, she picked him up at the airport, drove him home - to a house he had not been inside for two years - and helped him to get settled into a routine with the house and the botanical spoils of his divorce.

After receiving her degree in the Liberal Arts, Beryl tried to find a job with hours that would permit her to be home when her son came home from school each day. Her quest was daunting. Not only was a degree in Liberal Arts regarded as a 'negative' when considering an applicant's qualifications, (the choice of study having demonstrated a lack of foresight for eventual entry into the commercial job market) but by stipulating that she needed to be home no later than 3:30 p.m. each day, she further discouraged personnel managers from putting out their company's welcome mat. The supply of available jobs was somewhat limited.

Beryl, a Zen Buddhist and karate practitioner, was still doing part-time work when George proposed that they open a private investigation agency. Originally he had thought she would function as a "girl Friday" office manager; but when he witnessed her abilities in the martial arts, which, at that time, far exceeded his, he agreed that she should function as a 50-50 partner in the agency, and he helped her through the licensing procedure. She quickly became an excellent marksman on the gun range. As a Christmas gift he gave her a Beretta to use alternately with her Colt semi-automatic.

The Zen temple she attended was located on Germantown Avenue in a two storey, storefront row of small businesses. Wagner & Tilson, Private Investigators needed a home. Beryl noticed that a building in the same row was advertised for sale. She told George who liked it, bought it, and let Beryl and her son move into the second floor as their residence. Problem solved.

While George considered himself a man's man, Beryl did not see herself as a woman's woman. She had no female friends her own age. None. Acquaintances, yes. She enjoyed warm relationships with a few older women. But Beryl, it surprised her to realize, was a man's woman. She liked men, their freedom to move, to create, to discover, and that inexplicable wildness that came with their physical presence and strength. All of her senses found them agreeable; but she had no desire to domesticate one. Going to sleep with one was nice. But waking up with one of them in her bed? No. No. No. Dawn had an alchemical effect on her sensibilities. "Colors seen by candlelight do not look the same by day," said Elizabeth Barrett Browning, to which Beryl replied, "Amen."

She would find no occasion to alter her orisons until, in the course of solving a missing person's case that involved sexual slavery in a South American rainforest, a case called Skyspirit, she met the Surinamese Southern District's chief criminal investigator. Dawn became conducive to romance. But, as we all know, the odds are always against the success of long distance love affairs. To be stuck in one continent and love a man who is stuck in another holds as much promise for high romance as falling in love with Dorian Gray. In her professional life, she was tough but fair. In matters of lethality, she preferred dim mak points to bullets, the latter being awfully messy.

Perhaps the most unusual of the three detectives is Sensei Percy Wong. The reader may find it useful to know a bit more about his background.

Sensei, Beryl's karate master, left his dojo to go to Taiwan to become a fully ordained Zen Buddhist priest in the Ummon or Yun Men lineage in which he was given the Dharma name Shi Yao Feng. After studying advanced martial arts in both Taiwan and China, he returned to the U.S.

to teach karate again and to open a small Zen Buddhist temple - the temple that was down the street from the office *Wagner & Tilson* would eventually open.

Sensei was quickly considered a great martial arts' master not because, as he explains, "I am good at karate, but because I am better at advertising it." He was of Chinese descent and had been ordained in China, and since China's Chan Buddhism and Gung Fu stand in polite rivalry to Japan's Zen Buddhism and Karate, it was most peculiar to find a priest in China's Yun Men lineage who followed the Japanese Zen liturgy and the martial arts discipline of Karate.

It was only natural that Sensei Percy Wong's Japanese associates proclaimed that his preferences were based on merit, and in fairness to them, he did not care to disabuse them of this notion. In truth, it was Sensei's childhood rebellion against his tyrannical faux-Confucian father that caused him to gravitate to the Japanese forms. Though both of his parents had emigrated from China, his father decried western civilization even as he grew rich exploiting its freedoms and commercial opportunities. With draconian finesse he imposed upon his family the cultural values of the country from which he had fled for his life. He seriously believed that while the rest of the world's population might have come out of Africa, Chinese men came out of heaven. He did not know or care where Chinese women originated so long as they kept their proper place as slaves.

His mother, however, marveled at American diversity and refused to speak Chinese to her children, believing, as she did, in the old fashioned idea that it is wise to speak the language of the country in which one claims citizenship.

At every turn the dear lady outsmarted her obsessively sinophilic husband. Forced to serve rice at every meal along with other mysterious creatures obtained in Cantonese Chinatown, she purchased two Shar Peis that, being from Macau, were given free rein of the dining room. These dogs, despite their pre-Qin dynasty lineage, lacked a discerning palate and proved to be gluttons for bowls of fluffy white stuff. When her husband retreated to his rooms, she served omelettes and Cheerios, milk instead of tea, and at dinner, when he was not there at all, spaghetti instead of chow mein. The family home was crammed with gaudy enameled furniture and torturously carved teak; but on top of the lion-head-ball-claw-legged coffee table, she always placed a book which illustrated the elegant simplicity of such furniture designers as Marcel Breuer; Eileen Gray; Charles Eames; and American Shakers. Sensei adored her; and loved to hear her relate how, when his father ordered her to give their firstborn son a Chinese name; she secretly asked the clerk to record indelibly the name "Percy" which she mistakenly thought was a very American name. To Sensei, if she had named him Abraham Lincoln Wong, she could not have given him a more Yankee handle.

Preferring the cuisines of Italy and Mexico, Sensei avoided Chinese food and prided himself on not knowing a word of Chinese. He balanced this ignorance by an inability to understand Japanese and, because of its inaccessibility, he did not eat Japanese food.

The Man of Zen who practices Karate obviously is the adventurous type; and Sensei, staying true to type, enjoyed participating in Beryl's and George's investigations. It required little time for him to become a one-third partner of the team. He called himself, "the ampersand in *Wagner & Tilson*."

Sensei Wong may have been better at advertising karate than at performing it, but this merely says that he was a superb huckster for the discipline. In college he had studied civil engineering; but he also was on the fencing team and he regularly practiced gymnastics. He had learned yoga and ancient forms of meditation from his mother. He attained Zen's vaunted transcendental states; which he could access 'on the mat.' It was not surprising that when he began to learn karate he was already half-accomplished. After he won a few minor championships he attracted the attention of several martial arts publications that found his "unprecedented" switchings newsworthy. They imparted to him a "great master" cachet, and perpetuated it to the delight of dojo owners and martial arts shopkeepers. He did win many championships and, through unpaid endorsements and political propaganda, inspired the sale of Japanese weapons, including nunchaku and shuriken which he did not actually use.

Although his Order was strongly given to celibacy, enough wiggle room remained for the priest who found it expedient to marry or dally. Yet, having reached his mid-forties unattached, he regarded it as 'unlikely' that he would ever be romantically welded to a female, and as 'impossible' that he would be bonded to a citizen and custom's agent of the People's Republic of China - whose Gung Fu abilities challenged him and who would strike terror in his heart especially when she wore Manolo Blahnik red spike heels. Such combat, he insisted, was patently unfair, but he prayed that Providence would not level the playing field. He met his femme fatale while working on *A Case of Virga*.

Later in their association Sensei would take under his spiritual wing a young Thai monk who had a degree in computer science and a flair for acting. Akara Chatree, to whom Sensei's master in Taiwan would give the name Shi Yao Xin, loved Shakespeare; but his father - who came from one of Thailand's many noble families - regarded his son's desire to become an actor as we would regard our son's desire to become a hit man. Akara's brothers were all businessmen and professionals; and as the old patriarch lay dying, he exacted a promise from his tall 'matinee-idol' son that he would never tread upon the flooring of a stage. The old man had asked for nothing else, and since he bequeathed a rather large sum of money to his young son, Akara had to content himself with critiquing the performances of actors who were less filially constrained than he. As far as romance is concerned, he had not thought too much about it until he worked on *A Case of Industrial Espionage*. That case took him to Bermuda, and what can a young hero do when he is captivated by a pretty girl who can recite Portia's lines with crystalline insight while lying beside him on a white beach near a blue ocean?

But his story will keep...

WEDNESDAY, NOVEMBER 2, 2011

In 1835, Black Walnut Farm had been "built to last for a thousand years as a monument to beauty," or so the owner proclaimed at the building's dedication ceremony. The splendid house might have made it to one hundred had indoor plumbing and electricity not come along, for the eventual inclusion of these amenities disfigured every room. Delicately paneled walls and ceilings were scarred by electric wires, switches and plugs. Meticulously laid parquet floors were punctured to accommodate ugly water and sewage pipes. No one could find a way to incorporate patched add-ons into the house's esthetic integrity. No matter how competently a bathroom was designed and constructed, it still had a jury-rigged look about it.

Bathrooms, placed on either side of a non-load bearing wall, had their pipes accessible on only one side, and this by small wooden doors cut into the wall of the less important room.

Heidi Bielmann, the owner of Black Walnut Farm, slept too soundly to hear someone enter the adjoining bedroom, open the access door to her bathtub's pipes, and feed a white electrical cord through the aperture of her tub's hot water faucet. She also did not notice that the person who did this then entered her bedroom, tip-toed past her wheelchair, entered her bathroom, loosened the faucet's cover plate, and pulled the cord through until it descended to the safety drain. To conceal the electric cord, the person then took a long blue nylon ruffled 'back scrubber' and looped the end over the faucet. Having heard none of this, it was unlikely that she would be disturbed by the person's leaving, or by the cord's plug being inserted into an electrical outlet in the adjoining bedroom. When Heidi's body was lowered into the water for her morning bath, displacement would raise the water level more than enough for the water to make contact with the wire.

If the plan succeeded, by the time the morning sun reached its zenith, Black Walnut Farm would have a new owner.

The mailman routinely arrived at the storefront offices of Wagner & Tilson, Private Investigators, at ten o'clock in the morning. Depending on the mood he was in, he would follow the script of one of two announcements: either he would pretend to check the mail bag and say, "You didn't get notified from the Publisher's Clearing Sweepstakes that you're a winner today. But you're still the stars of my route. I'd ask you for your autographs but you didn't get any certified mail, either." Or, he'd feign confusion about whether the mail addressed to "occupant," "resident," and "To the Folks at" had reached the correct recipient. Real Mail and mail addressed specifically to Beryl Tilson who lived on the second floor of the building, he would carefully place in the center of Beryl's desk in the outer office.

Beryl was not in the office on the cold November day that the 'stand-up' mailman brought the stiff white cardboard envelope that bore the "do not fold - contains photographs" warning on it. George Wagner was standing near the front door when the mailman arrived and this particular envelope was on top of the entire mail collection. George saw it immediately and his expression made the mailman cancel whichever performance he had intended to give. He handed it to George who carried it back into his office. The mailman put the rest of the mail on Beryl's desk and left.

George, who had once received a commendation for engaging in a gun fight with three armed burglars, (leaving two dead and one wounded), trembled at the sight of the girlish handwriting. He fumbled with the flap, trying to pull the 'tear strip' back, and when he couldn't get his fingers around the end tab, he took a box cutter and drew the blade across the top edge until the two sides parted and he could reach in and extract two photographs and a long handwritten letter.

The photographs were of Lilyanne Smith and the letter was written by her. In both photos she wore the same black sweater and had her natural curly blonde hair similarly arranged. Lilyanne Smith was a former client who had been victimized in a cruel swindle; and George, having felt a special fondness for the girl, had given her the key to his house so that in an emergency she would have a safe place to go. He hadn't intended that she wear it around her neck, suspended by a long gold chain; yet, he had to admit that it looked like a gold pendant of some kind that belonged exactly where it was. In both photographs her arms were folded and rested on a table; but in one her expression was dour and she wore an engagement ring, and in the other she was smiling broadly and there was no ring on her finger. He turned this photograph over and read the back: *"For George in all his aliases. The key is to the door of my heart's panic room. With much love, Lily."*

Before he could open the letter that accompanied the photographs, the office door opened and Mr. and Mrs. Hiram Bielmann entered and shouted, "Anybody here?"

George shoved the envelope, letter, and photographs into his desk drawer and answered, "Yes. Come on in!" He got up and walked to the front office to greet them.

Loreen and Hiram Bielmann, red nosed and shivering, were pleasant despite having walked two blocks from the closest parking place they could find. They were well dressed and otherwise graceful in their movements. George smiled. "I can see you had to walk a distance. If I knew you were coming I'd have told you that you could park here behind the office. How can I help you?" he asked.

"We called last night," Hiram said, "and left a message asking you to let us know if it was all right if we dropped by at 10 a.m. I explained that we had to attend a funeral this morning and naturally we had to keep our phones off. When we left the church, we checked our messages and didn't hear any objection."

George was embarrassed. "That's my fault. I didn't pick up my messages. But it's cold outside and warm in here and I've got two comfortable chairs for you to sit on back in my office. And since my health-conscious partner has taken me off coffee and put me on tea, I'll make a pot of jasmine. How does that sound?"

They said that it sounded fine and made themselves comfortable in his office.

Loreen and Hiram smoked brown cigarettes, the nearly five inch long brand. George hadn't smoked in years, but he still kept an ashtray on his desk though at the moment it was filled with paper clips. He prepared the tea and brought the pot and tea tray into his office just in time for them to crush their butts in the saucers of the porcelain cups. He asked Mrs. Bielmann to serve the tea while he nuked a plate of butter cookies.

"Now," he asked, "what is the problem that brought you here on this cold day?"

Hiram Bielmann paused to scratch his beard. "We've never dealt with a private investigator before. I must apologize in advance for any clumsiness we exhibit in telling our story. One tends to despise oneself for bringing an action against a mentally ill family member."

The office phone rang. "We'll let it go to voice-mail," George said, grinning. "Why set a precedent?"

"Fate," said Hiram Bielmann with philosophical gravitas, "can cause the most innocent of actions to bring financial ruin to one's household." He then spoiled the effect by flipping open his gold cigarette lighter and sucking the flame into a second cigarette. He exhaled and resumed his observations about Fate. "I was married before. My late former wife and I had two children, James and Heidi. She... my late former wife... had one of those mental afflictions that don't show themselves until it is too late. Before you realize that your mate is genetically flawed, you've already had children and the affliction has been passed on. When my son James was sixteen he went to a 'Potter's Field' graveyard - the kind with numbered plaques for those who died without having been identified - and he committed suicide. At the time, Heidi who was then eighteen, was also showing signs of the disease that afflicts her now. She sought refuge in religion."

Loreen Bielmann decided to make a contribution to the discussion. "Yes," she sighed, "heredity is everything. You can argue 'nature versus nurture' all you want. Nature will prevail." She stared at her tea, willing it to become cool enough to drink.

Hiram continued, "My daughter Heidi, evidencing the depth of her mental illness, has initiated a series of abusive actions against us. She desperately needs psychotherapy but naturally she refuses to get it. In order to force her commitment to a hospital, we need proof of her mental incompetence. We consulted our family attorney, V. Bruce Galeen, he recommended that we seek Wagner & Tilson's help - and here we are."

George nodded. "Galeen's a good man," he said. He had never heard of the attorney, or if he had, he couldn't remember him. "A very good man."

Hiram resumed his narrative. "My late former wife and I divorced after she became a raging bull. I'm ashamed to admit that while I understood her disease, I simply couldn't tolerate it. I was driven to give her whatever she wanted to sever our ties - and that included Black Walnut Farm - our estate. She returned to her family home in Colorado, leaving our daughter Heidi alone to grieve for her brother. Naturally, I stayed on at BW to comfort her and to help her to prepare for convent life. Heidi intended to become a nun.

"My late former wife's family is extremely wealthy. They didn't need Black Walnut, but spite acts irrespective of need. After Heidi entered the convent, I was alone in the house until I met and married this wonderful woman," he reached for Loreen's hand and squeezed it. "This dear lady brought four wonderful children to our union. I consider them my children even though their biological father refuses to allow me to adopt them formally. Their ages are seventeen, fifteen, eleven and nine." Bielmann again squeezed his wife's hand. "The two boys are the bookends... the two girls are in the middle.

"For the first time that I could recall, life at Black Walnut was joyful. Then, as luck would have it, my late former wife suddenly died. She left everything to Heidi.

"Eighteen months ago Heidi left Saint Catherine's and came back to Black Walnut—"

"Saint Catherine's?" George could not let the reference pass. Lilyanne Smith had also been at Saint Catherine's in West Virginia.

"Yes, a cloistered order of nuns in West Virginia. She left two years before she would have taken her final vows. We could see why she left the convent. Her illness had surfaced. She went from ill-tempered to agitated to angry to suspicious to paranoid. The decline was dreadful... dreadful! She cancelled my access to the estate's accounts. She wanted us to leave; but we knew she needed care. We couldn't leave her alone in that big place," he sighed. "She actually started eviction proceedings and became devious in her hatefulness. We weren't worried about having a roof over our heads because Loreen owned a substantial property. True, it was heavily mortgaged. Four children can be expensive to raise! But then... then." He fell silent, quashed temporarily by the burden of Fate.

Loreen nodded. "Black Walnut wasn't enough! She also inherited a company that bought debts. They purchased our mortgage and demanded that we make one large payment to cover arrears. We asked Heidi to lend us the money to pay her. She refused. The house was sold at auction and she bought it to give to her lover's wife."

The story was becoming bizarre. George blinked. "What? A nun left Saint Catherine's convent to take a married man as her lover and forced her stepmother's house into foreclosure so that she could buy it and give it to her lover's wife?"

"Oh, yesssss," Loreen hissed. "The stableman's *son* is her lover. He moved into her bedroom. Then she moved the *stableman* into his own bedroom on the same floor with us. Think of our two daughters! Is this not insane?"

"It's certainly a challenging lifestyle," George said, unable to find another description for it.

"But that's not our problem," Hiram said judiciously. "Her morality is not for us to judge. What we cannot ignore, however, is her fanaticism about faith healing. Her lover, Timmy Michelson, has a wife who has an incurable *inherited* affliction - *polycystic kidney disease*. The poor woman is impoverished and has no alternative but to rely on God's help. She and Tim are avid believers in faith healing. And this would be none of our concern, either, but he has indoctrinated Heidi with these fantastic beliefs. Some months ago, Heidi was riding alone while Tim was shopping in town. When he got back he found her saddled horse standing in the paddock. It was a very mysterious accident. I insisted that he take her to the hospital. Instead, he took her to one of those first-aid clinics. They wanted to transfer her to a real hospital, but she refused. She wanted to use Tim's faith healers. She had injured her spine, but despite donating a fortune to those charlatans, she's still in a wheelchair."

"And Bruce Galeen wants her behavior documented? What other hateful or eccentric behavior has she shown?" George asked.

Loreen answered. "Old Mr. Michelson coughs and coughs. It could be tuberculosis for all we know. I begged her. I told her that as long as she purchased my home for a song she might as well let Tim Michelson's father live in it. It is dangerous to have a person with a respiratory disease living among healthy people. And on top of this, there is the horrendous stress it puts me under. Hiram and I have been trying for four years to have a child of our own. We know that God helps those who help themselves. I faithfully use an ovulation kit and fertility monitor. I eat properly and get the right amount of exercise and rest. We would have wonderful children! I am good maternal stock. My four children prove it. And this great man here is such a wonderful father!" Loreen sighed as Hiram squeezed her shoulder. She picked up a butter cookie and nibbled on it. When she finished, she began to stroke Hiram's knee and seemed to be wiping some of the oil from the cookies on his pants. Hiram stared at her hand which she removed and then began to caress a paper napkin.

She continued. "Tim puts his kids in a day nursery - which Heidi pays for, naturally. Tim sleeps with Heidi... dines with Heidi... rides with Heidi. His wife is dying and he's cantering like a gentleman. Breeches and boots. His poor wife learned about the affair. Not only was she losing her life, she was losing her husband, and quite probably had passed the kidney disease on to her children. She became a wild woman! All I could think about was Mr. Rochester's wife in *Jane Eyre*. I'm telling you... there were nights I couldn't sleep I was so worried that his wife would come by and burn the house down around us... use the pages of a Bible for kindling.

"We insisted that Tim and his father not spend another night in our home! We were ignored."

George looked up. "And you think that perhaps Tim's wife is capable of causing fatal accidents to exact some kind of retribution?"

Loreen lit a cigarette. "She's desperate! And I ask you... have you ever heard of the stableman sleeping on the same floor as–" she gestured towards Hiram, "–the master of the house?" She took a deep drag on her cigarette and 'french-inhaled' it. George was fascinated to see the smoke leave her lips and get sucked up into her nose. Hiram watched George watch Loreen and a faint look of satisfaction flickered across his face. George, he thought, had been 'hooked' by his beautiful wife.

"I see," George said with a slight smile that reinforced Hiram's suspicion. "Your daughters now must share what should be an intimate family environment with two male servants. I understand your concern."

Loreen continued. "Tim and Heidi go to faith healing meetings. And it is one donation after the other. And it is never enough. The quacks always need more money! She could give them a donation every day from now until the sun becomes a red giant and it wouldn't be enough."

Hiram held his wife's hand. "Do you see our problem?" he asked George. "My daughter wants to throw her family out on the street while she squanders money on servants and faith healers. If Tim Michelson's wife should die - and she is extremely ill - Heidi will marry him. And he will control her entire estate. She is physically and mentally unable to care for herself or her financial affairs. And that is why we are here, today.

"Our attorney says that we need proof. Please... can you help us to convince a court that my daughter is not competent to manage her affairs?"

George sighed. "Of course I'll look into the case. I'd like to get inside the house to see what surveillance opportunities there are. What you capture on film can lead you to other even more convincing proofs of her incompetence. To get in the house I'll need a cover story. Have you any suggestions... am I a friend or relative... a business associate?"

The office door opened with an urgent quickness. Sensei Percy Wong, the Zen Buddhist priest who often worked with them on cases, came directly back to George's office. "I'm sorry to interrupt," he said, "but an emergency has come up. George, could I speak with you in private for a moment?"

George got up and followed Sensei into the front office and then, to his surprise, out onto the street. "What's up?"

"Do you never check your messages? Lilyanne is frantic. She sent you a letter of some kind and is afraid you won't get it in time."

"I got it. In time for what?"

"She wrote to warn you that her friend Heidi Bielmann's father is trying to have her declared incompetent. They're going to try to enlist you to help them. Lily wanted to warn you not to believe a word they said. She called me when she couldn't reach Beryl or you. She found out this morning that they were on their way here. The Bielmanns are broke and will do anything to get money. Lily said she thinks they're trying to kill Heidi - something about a riding accident. Heidi needs your help. So you should go along with them and agree to help them and then call her. Were those people in your office the Bielmanns?"

"Yes... Jesus. I almost signed a contract with them."

Sensei had to return to the temple, but George held his arm. "I've got an ethical problem here," George said more to himself than to Sensei. "But call Lily back and tell her that she may have gotten to me too late. Tell her I'll call her within the hour."

George returned to his office, completely confused about what he was supposed to do and how he was going to reject these people as clients and then show up as Heidi's agent.

As he apologized for the interruption and sat again at his desk, the only constructive thought that formed in his mind was that the cookies were buttery and would leave good prints on whatever they touched. He could get DNA from the butts or tea cups. He did not know what use any of this would be, but it at least seemed constructive.

It was bath time. Heidi Bielmann wasn't sure that her father and stepmother had left the house. They often went through the motions of leaving only to sneak back in to spy on her with their camera phones, hoping to catch her doing something that was inimical to their well-being or to hers, if they could prove it.

Hiram and Loreen suspected that Heidi's "wheelchair dramatics" were both a sympathy-gaining ploy designed to thwart them in a court proceeding and a faith-healer's trick that would be performed at a time that would give maximum exposure to the claim of miraculous cure. They were not sure, however, for whose benefit Heidi was pretending to be disabled. They had tried to bribe her servants, but they had no money, and the servants remained loyal their employer. In fact, Heidi was not in the least disabled. By claiming to require physical assistance she was able to keep Tim Michelson on the premises as a "paid caregiver." When her father and Loreen were out of the house, she would get up and walk normally.

Gertrude, her chambermaid and assistant, picked up the breakfast tray. "I'll ask cook if they've gone out. If she doesn't know, I'll check the cars in front and in the garage. I checked their bedroom. They're not in there. Mrs. Gomez wants to vacuum the bedrooms while the kids are still at school. She said to ask you if you planned to go back to sleep."

Heidi picked up the morning paper. "No, I'm awake for the day. My friend, Miss Lilyanne Smith, will be here for lunch. Tell Mrs. Gomez to go ahead with her cleaning, and ask cook to make something special for Miss L and me for lunch in the enclosed patio. Mr. Michelson will be here for dinner. The weather report is good. I'll have dinner for him, me, and the two children served also in the enclosed patio."

Tim Michelson usually did not stay at Black Walnut Farm on Tuesday nights. He would pick his two children up at day school on Tuesday afternoon and take them home to have a pizza dinner with his wife and her mother. After dinner he would take his wife to their faith healing church while her mother watched the children and then he would spend the night at home with them. On Wednesdays, he would stay with his wife and children until mid-afternoon; and then he would return with the children to Black Walnut Farm. Often, he would also spend Friday and Saturday nights at home. On the weekends, if his wife felt strong enough, he would take her and the children to the movies or the shopping mall.

Gertrude returned with the news that Mr. and Mrs. Bielmann were definitely gone. "Cook says they went to attend a funeral in Philadelphia. They're not expected back until after lunch." She asked if she should fill the tub. Heidi said she'd wait until Miss Lilyanne phoned and then she'd take her bath.

Mrs. Gomez pushed the vacuum cleaner into the bedroom beside Heidi's. She went to plug it in and found a white cord in the outlet. The cord went into the door in the wall. "Where does this go?" she called.

Gertrude stopped in the hallway. "Where does what go?"

"This cord... I've never seen it before. It goes into the plumbing door."

Gertrude looked. "That's odd," she said, opening the door. She traced the wire until it disappeared into the pipes that led into the other room. "Unplug it!" she ordered. "Let's see where this goes."

She hurried around to Heidi's bedroom and entered the bathroom. "Something's funny," she said to Heidi. She could see the cord behind the blue nylon scrubby. "My God!" she shouted. "This was an attempt on your life!" It then occurred to Gertrude that she often lowered Heidi into the water - that meant she would be physically connected to her! "On both our lives! Get Mr. Michelson!"

The old stableman shuffled down the hall in his bedroom slippers and bathrobe. He examined the cord, the scrubby, the cover plate in Heidi's tub. Then he went into the next bedroom and Mrs. Gomez showed him where the plug had been inserted into the outlet. Soberly, he returned to Heidi's room, carrying the cord. "When Gertrude lowered you into the water, the two of you would have been electrocuted. We should call the police."

"No," Heidi said. "Let's wait until Lily and Tim are here." She began to cry. "My own father!"

"Miss Heidi," Gertrude said solemnly, "your reluctance to get tough with those people is now putting my life at risk, too. Either you act or I'll be forced to quit. I have a family to take care of."

"Give me a day. Lily will know what to do."

Loreen Bielmann smiled at George in a conspiratorial intimacy. "So you need to get into the house and see Heidi in action and decide what will be the best way to get proof of her craziness?"

"Yes, but mostly to see if I'd recommend the services of a security expert. These experts and their high-tech hidden electronics are usually expensive, so it's best to see if we really need them. I'll need a cover."

"I have an idea. Why don't you come as a faith healer? Dress up like one of these spiritual quacks. Are you familiar enough with the Bible to pull it off?"

"You know," George said, "that's one great idea! But faith healers come in all religions. Since she's already a member of a Christian community, I can go as a yogi or swami. She may be more agreeable to trying a different approach. I can say I was sent by a friend who wishes to remain anonymous." He got out two copies of an agency contract and handed one to Hiram, while he continued to speak to Loreen. "Let your husband look over the contract. Now, as I see it, the best way to handle this is on a limited objective contract. In other words, I'll contract with you to do a specific job, and then, when you evaluate the results, you can decide what course you want to take, and we'll draft a new limited objective contract for whatever specific goal you have in mind. Our first task is to determine the surveillance environment, and the ease with which cameras can get close enough to Miss Bielmann's bedroom and other areas she frequents with her lover. This, as I've said will be expensive. But you, dear lady, have come up with a great idea." Before he began to fill in the blank spaces in his copy of the contract, he looked up and asked, "How will you be paying for this? Our fee is a thousand dollars a day... plus expenses. The surveillance installations will be done by another firm under separate contract."

The Bielmanns looked at each other. Loreen Bielmann crushed her cigarette in the saucer. "We were rather hoping that you'd accept a percentage of the money we receive when the court decides to declare Heidi incompetent. The problems we're having with the girl have cut off our funds. We simply cannot afford such an outlay of cash at this time."

"Unfortunately," said George, relieved although he affected a disappointed expression, "I have partnership agreements that forbid accepting a case without being paid a retainer... and this case might require a week to complete. Naturally, we'll refund any monies that are not spent on the project. But I cannot break our agency's rules. A partnership has to be strict about giving free advice or favors to friends and relatives." He directed his gaze to the diamond rings Loreen was wearing and made a suggestion that he knew would never be considered. "Perhaps madam has a piece of jewelry she could pawn with the understanding that the pawnshop will hold it longer before offering it for sale. And then she can purchase the jewelry back when she receives the money."

The Bielmanns did not want to pawn their jewelry or anything of value that they still owned. It was clear to George that they did not intend to pay at all.

"Really," Hiram Bielmann said, "can't we work something out? It would be not only for the sake of my daughter Heidi, but for my other four children, too."

"Well," said George, "perhaps there is merit in not creating the bonds of agency." George couldn't imagine trying to explain in a courtroom that he was acting as the paid agent of people he was actually working against. "I'll tell you what," he continued, "since it was Bruce Galeen who recommended me, I'll look into the problem as a consideration to him. I'll go to the house in the guise of a faith healer, but it must be clearly understood that I am in no way acting as your agent. But frankly, if I am acting independently of you... legally... the evidence I uncover will be worth more in any court. Set your mind at ease and verify this with Bruce. I'll simply visit Heidi in the guise of a faith healer. Naturally, I can't accept money," he winked, "since that would be practicing medicine without a license. I'll go to the house completely independent of you and your interests."

"Perfect!" Loreen Bielmann's fingers were jubilant. She pushed back the agency papers with her sculptured nails. "And you can be sure that when we win our case, we will reward you handsomely. But time is of the essence. Could you possibly come this Saturday?"

George consulted his desk calendar. "Saturday, November 5th. That would give me a few days to obtain the proper garments... let's say, of a Hindu faith healer. How does that sound?"

"Excellent!" Hiram said. "Here's a plan. Come by in the morning. Loreen and I will act as if we're opposed to your visit. Naturally, Heidi will insist that you be admitted. Spitefulness is a symptom of her illness. That is the unfortunate way we live these days."

"I'll call at the house at ten o'clock in the morning. I'll figure out a way to get upstairs to her bedroom... a private interview or examination. We'll make it work!"

Bielmann stood up and George extended his good left hand to shake hands. It was awkward and he and Bielmann exchanged a friendly laugh. Mrs. Bielmann insisted on shaking his hand, too. "Friends?" she asked.

"Right," replied George. "We have no legal connection or obligation whatsoever. But if I have to call you on the phone I'll say I'm a friend of Hiram's from the club...?"

"The *Ottowami*."

"Ah, I know the place. *The Ottowami Men's Social Retreat*. It's in Media."

"Exactly."

"All right then. Fortunately I'm not busy now... it's that time of year when things of this nature usually slow down. If you had come in January, Bruce Galeen or no Bruce Galeen, I'd never be able to arrange it."

As soon as they left, he took the cups and contract copies back into the kitchen. Later on he'd decide if he still wanted to retain them for fingerprint and DNA data. Meanwhile, he had Lily's letter to attend to. He returned to his desk and removed the envelope, letter, and Lily's happy photograph which he propped against his desk lamp.

He held the letter which had been written on legal size tablet paper to his nose. He could smell her perfume. Maybe, he thought, she was perspiring a little when she wrote it. He remembered the scent.

My Dearest George,

I am writing to you now to tell you two things. One is about me and my mysterious love life and the other, which I'll begin with, is about a dear lady-friend-girl (I never know how to refer to a fellow ex-novice) who was in Saint Catherine's convent with me. She left the Order before I did and didn't know that I had gone out into the world and was now so experienced and well connected. (I am laughing and have to stop writing... forgive me... one moment, please.)

All right... I have collected my wits. I promise to restrain myself since her problem is serious. Naturally, when she heard last winter about my brilliant engagement to a French nobleman, - ok ok I'm laughing so hard now that I can't continue writing. Oh Lord... it has taken me... what? three seconds to break another vow? I'll try again...

When she saw that announcement she assumed that by now I was married and probably a pregnant queen of something. Then a couple of weeks ago she saw the enclosed photo of me wearing an engagement ring and the announcement that I was engaged to Reverend Forbes deBurry Snyder, IV. Last week she read that the engagement had been broken and she naturally suspected that my love life was as screwed up as hers. Hah...

My friend from the convent, Heidi Bielmann, is twenty-four. She's cursed with ten times more money than I have. She has good reason to suspect that she is being targeted for hers. She's in love with a good guy; but marriage for them, at least in the foreseeable future, is impossible. But trouble has already arrived.

Her father and his wife are trying to get her declared non compos mentis. They made an appointment with the family lawyer to initiate the action. But that attorney is her mother's family attorney; and she knew he couldn't take the case because of a conflict of interest. She talked to me and I told her to call him and to suggest that he let his secretary recommend those great private investigators, Wagner and Tilson, for their consideration (since they would need evidence to support their claim). She did and the secretary did and if her father follows through, you should be hearing from him and/or his wife. Please take my word for it, Heidi is not nuts and her father and his wife are evil. Beyond that I will not try to influence your judgment.

Now... to return to the reason I had the second photo taken... just for you...

I had just gotten home from my "world humiliation tour" (my mother thought that if we hid out in Borneo, Patagonia, and Diego Garcia for a year or so, people might forget my horrific winter engagement), when an acquaintance of my mother's dropped by with her son, Forbes deBurry Snyder, IV, to look at our orchids. She was like a bulldozer and he was like a violet growing in her path. Anyway, Forbes deBurry Snyder IV asked me to show him the hothouse. I agreed and this evidently committed me to bear Forbes deBurry Snyder V. I didn't understand the full extent of his agenda. (I'm easily confused, as you know.) Forbes deBurry Snyder, IV is getting his doctorate in theology at Yale. Forbes deBurry Snyder, IV took me to the art museum and gave me one perfect rose for my 24th birthday (my dad wondered why 'two dozen' did not suggest itself to him); and while you may find this difficult to believe, Forbes deBurry Snyder, IV pinned a corsage of gardenias on me when he took me to a musical review, a Lutheran version of a Rave. The music was by a string quartet and an accappella choir. Fun? You becha'.

But anyway, Forbes deBurry Snyder, IV told my father that we were in love - (we meaning him and me, not me and you). (Aargh! wrong case!) Naturally he wanted me to grace his table or some such piece of furniture. He said that he knew the integrity of his Christian mission was so inviolable that everyone would know that no Man Of The Cloth, such as he, would ever give his name to 'damaged goods.' And then he showed my father an old filigree 1/2 carat engagement ring which he said had been given to an ancestress of his some two hundred years ago. The ring had been passed down to all the deBurry wives of the oldest son ever since. I get goose pimples just thinking about it. I mean... I'd get to be in a lineup! Turns the cop in you on, doesn't it? Confess...

Since my mother went to school with his mother and since he was wearing a clerical collar, my dear Dad invited Forbes deBurry Snyder, IV and Mrs. Forbes deBurry Snyder, III to our house for dinner the following week. I told my Dad to count me out. He and my mother wanted to discuss it but I explained that I was too busy looking for someplace else to be on that particular evening. "Be honest and tell him yourself how you are not ready yet, and so on," my astute parents insisted. So I attended the dinner and refused the ring but he insisted that I at least try it on "to see if it fit" and his mother took that cellphone photograph. He wouldn't take the ring back. I had to test drive it for a few days. But the next day his mother called some society editor and news of our engagement "just happened to slip out."

Taking a page from *The Textbook of Love* by Wagner & Tilson, P.I.'s, I immediately took the ring to the biggest pawn shop I could find and paid the owner to research the bauble. He called me back in a couple of days. I went back to the shop and saw a lovely photo of it... it had been stolen in 2005 from some unfortunate lady in Hartford, Connecticut. He said that he was obliged to call the police. I said, "Please do." I had called Daddy's secretary and asked her to look into their financial background. As expected, they are in desperate need of cash, bonds, stocks, assets fixed and liquid... stuff like that. The police still hadn't picked them up for questioning when FdeBS, IV called my Dad seeking a dowry that would keep Manhattan in cocktails from now 'til the sun becomes a Red Giant. My Dad told him that the police had the ring and that he should try to get it back for the sake of the next Forbes deBurry Snyder and all the others that were sure to follow. Overcome with joy, I had Sanford take that second photo of me wearing the same sweater and in the same pose - just for your blue eyes only. Sanford says to send you his regards. Thus endeth my latest foray into the matrimonial wars.

(I am in constant touch with Margaret Cioran of Seattle. I don't think you ever met Margaret. She was my predecessor with Henri. Please tell Beryl she's safely out of rehab. I'll be seeing her, Jack, and Groff over the Christmas holidays.)

I hope all is well with you. Do I have to tell you how much I miss you?

Your Lily.

George re-read the letter half a dozen times and studied the second photograph. He tried to call Lily but his call went to voice-mail. He left no message. He poured a cold cup of tea and attended to what had been on his mind for the last hour. He munched on a cookie and smiled at Lilyanne's picture. Then he got out a notepad and wrote:

You sent your photo in the mail.
Did you think I needed it?
Did you think a bit of glossy paper -
A document of features -
Would help me to remember
Your eyes, hair, nose and mouth,
And that by wearing a high collar
I'd be cued to recall your Chaneled neck
And search my memory
For a scent I tossed in some olfactory bin?

Send instead a copy of your birth certificate.
Remind me - since I need to be reminded every day -
That I am twenty years older than you.

Older and old. Stale, worn out, used up.
Lost in the wonder of how it would feel
To have you beside me... in a warm bed, on a cold night.

I thank you for the photograph.
The gesture is appreciated... but not needed.

Your image is a solid figure that leaps from my eyes
Each time I close them.

It runs its fingers through my hair
And pushes its nose up under my chin
Or lets its lips tease my ear... whispering.

It puts its face next to mine
And rubs its silken skin against the stubble on my cheeks.
The friction generates a current
That turns my spine into a tesla coil.

I feel you in my arms and I fondle you with all my senses as a miser fondles gold. No, I do not need a photograph to remind me of what I alone know I own. There is not a cell in your body upon which my brain has not planted its flag.

He read the lines several times, tore the page from the pad, crumpled it into a ball, walked to the bathroom, and flushed it down the toilet.

He returned to his desk and attended to Loreen Bielmann's "coincidental" use of the same metaphor that Lilyanne had used - *Until the sun becomes a red giant*. This duplication of an unusual figure of speech indicated a strong possibility that Lilyanne's conversations with Heidi had been bugged. He tried again to call Lily and this time he left a message, "Before you talk to another person, call me. It's urgent."

As he returned to his desk, Lilyanne called. "I just got your message. I am honor-bound to keep my phone turned off while I'm driving. Yes, driving. I now am a licensed driver."

"Where are you now? And no goofing-off. This is serious."

"On my way to Black Walnut Farm... Heidi Bielmann's house. I'm stopped for a funeral procession, so I called you. I'm not allowed to talk and drive. We have to talk fast."

"Let me know when the traffic resumes. I think Heidi's phones are bugged. I want to ask you a question. It's serious so don't get silly. In your letter to me you used an expression, 'until the sun becomes a red giant.' Think back carefully. When did you use or hear someone else use that expression last?"

"Hmmm. I used it when I talked to Heidi yesterday. I said it in connection with marrying The Reverend Forbes et cetera. He could ask me to marry him every day from now until hell freezes or the sun becomes a red giant - whichever comes first, and my answer would still be 'No!' Something like that."

"When and where was she when you two spoke?"

"She was in her bedroom at Black Walnut Farm. She had to be in her bedroom because she was telling me about a new down quilt she had just spilled tea on."

"Land line or cellphone... and where were you when you told her about engaging me?"

"I don't think Heidi has a cellphone. They get a signal but it's not reliable. She's also afraid Loreen's kids would steal her phone and harass the people she calls. I was home in my room when I called her. When I was there and talked about you, we were outside in the garden."

"Good. They are probably bugging the phone or have a listening device in her bedroom. That 'red giant' line is unusual and it's witty. There's two ways to consider Loreen's use of the line. In a normal conversation, if one person uses a clever expression, the other person may consciously adopt it. We know it's conscious because he uses it selectively. He won't use it when he's talking to the person from whom he first heard it and he'll usually wait a bit before he uses it. So she might not connect me in any way with Heidi and therefore, selectively, feel free to plagiarize the line. Or else, when a person is intensely listening to something, say, a secretly made and scratchy recording, he might unconsciously adopt an unusual word or figure of speech. He'll spontaneously blurt it out at any time and he might even assume that he created the line.

"All right," he said, "here's what happened. They showed up here around ten o'clock. They said they left a message last night, but I didn't pick up my messages. They didn't want to sign an agency agreement and I said I couldn't proceed without the required retainer. I said maybe it was just as well. Since the eminent Bruce Galeen had recommended me, I would go out there on Saturday morning in the guise of a faith healer and check out Heidi's behavior and look over the surveillance environment. However, I wanted it clearly understood that I could not be functioning as their agent. They were thrilled. And, yes, in my opinion your friend is in serious trouble."

"I know. Somebody tampered with her wheelchair. Her motorized wheelchair was in the repair shop and they got an old wicker wheelchair from up in the attic for her to use. Somehow the wheel managed to fall off as Tim was taking her down the outside steps that lead to the stables. The chair tipped over but she wasn't hurt. Then there was that riding accident - that was no accident. They're getting desperate."

"If she's in physical danger then you ought to stay away from her house. Don't give me more to worry about. Call me later when you can talk. I'll dictate a script for Heidi to follow when I get out there as a Swami of some kind."

"A swami! I'm excited! But pick up your phone when I call!"

"Yes, dear. Make sure you have a pencil and paper ready. Drive carefully!"

He smiled as he disconnected the call.

George made a few notes and quickly answered his desk phone when it rang. "I'm ready," Lilyanne said. "I had to get gas so I stopped into the little cafeteria. I am now your official secretary."

"Heidi should never discuss anything on her house phones. I'll be there around 10 a.m. Saturday morning, dressed like an Indian swami. The Bielmanns have agreed to vigorously oppose allowing me in the house; but Heidi must insist that I be admitted. She should say that she knows me by reputation and that she trusts me to help cure her spine, and so on. I'll need to get up into Heidi's bedroom to see what surveillance equipment they've got in place and to decide where we'll be installing the equipment she needs if she wants to prove that they're trying to harm her. They don't own the house and so they can't legally bug the phones or secretly video the interior.

"Heidi is not to talk or write to anyone - by anyone I include Tim - about this arrangement. Michelson may be the greatest guy in the world, but he could also say something innocently that will jeopardize the operation. She can tell him later that she was acting to protect him. Get her out of the house when you speak to her. They probably have the whole place bugged. They will do whatever it takes to get something on her that will support their case."

"Got it," Lily said.

"When you see her again, get the names of her family members... place and date of birth. Call Beryl with the information if you can't reach me.

"All right. I'm an American swami, from Milwaukee, Wisconsin; but I'm called Swami Swahananda. Beryl has a book by some guy with a name like that. I learned faith healing from some world famous faith healer, and I am not going to charge for my services. I was sent there by a benefactor who must remain anonymous.

"Heidi has to play this absolutely straight. For as long as we are inside the house, I'm going to be the faith healer and she's going to be the patient. Everything depends on the Bielmanns not suspecting that she is in on the charade. She should ask me if I want to conduct any kind of examination on her spine. I'll say that it would be helpful but I don't want to make her feel uncomfortable in any way. She should say that so many strangers have looked at her back that she's immune to embarrassment... something like that. And she should take me up to her bedroom so that I can see her spine and have a look around. And she should affirm her strong belief that she can be cured by faith. Do you have all that? The Bielmanns may be standing there and I want her to say the right things."

Lily said that she understood. "Can I be there when you come as a faith healer?"

"No. Absolutely not. Don't even think about it."

"You are so mean to me. I want to see you be a swami!"

"When I'm a swami, I'm working as a swami. Someday when you need a faith healer, I may show up. Tell me something. Hiram said that Heidi filed eviction papers months ago. How come he and Loreen and the kids are still there?"

"They did some legal maneuvering, but the main reason is that they took some photographs of Tim and Heidi in bed and threaten to create a scandal. They'll cause as much pain as they can for Tim's family. Heidi can't permit that."

"I figured as much. Ok. Tell her to be circumspect in her conversations."

"Yes, Mr. Wagner. I will and I'll repeat what I said earlier. Now pay attention. I said that I keep my cellphone off when I'm driving. Did your Minx say, 'Drive'? Yes, she did. And you have no response to that news? I thought you'd be so proud of me. I can even parallel park. Do you miss me?"

"Like I miss a toothache."

"Do you know that I haven't danced since the day you taught me?"

"Whose fault is that? Mine?"

"You are a beast."

"Sometimes a man has to be a beast. It's been nice talking to you but I have prepare to be a faith healer."

"Oh... I want to see!"

"Good by-yai...."

When his heart slowed down to reasonably normal limits, he wolfed down the remaining cookies, locked the office and went down the street to the temple to get Sensei's help with the swami presentation. Sensei Percy Wong would know how to act and dress the part.

"You? A faith-healer?" Sensei said. It was the response George expected when he described the assignment.

"Yes. I'm going to heal by faith alone... and I don't have much time. Where do I get the duds to look like a faith healer and how do I say faith-healing things?"

Sensei was studying himself in the temple's kitchen mirror, "I think I look younger when I've got hair."

"We all do, Percy. Now... help me with this faith-healing business. I need to be believable by Saturday morning."

"Fortunately," said Sensei, "we don't have faith-healers in Zen... at least that I know of. And if you know of one, keep it to yourself. Let's go down to the Indian flea market and get you proper clothing from Kashmir. I'll drive. You can take notes when you ask me about attitudes and phrases you should use."

"When we're driving, I'll call Beryl and ask her to go out to Media to check the reference library."

"Hmmm," Sensei said quietly. "So you're Swami Swahananda, the renowned faith healer. Did I tell you about this crick I've got in my back between my shoulder blades?"

As they walked through the aisles of the flea market George's ring tone played *Nessun Dorma*, his affirmation that telephone calls disturb people.

Sensei stopped walking. "Answer it!" he barked at George. "Jesus, you tell me you promised Lily–"

"–All right! George would have preferred to take the call in private. He pulled his phone from his pocket and fumbled with it to take the call. Lily, too frantic to speak clearly, launched a string of syllables that George could not understand. Sensei took the phone from his hand.

"Lily, this is Perce... slow down. You're too excited. Speak more clearly. What's wrong?"

"This morning," Lily began, "the housekeeper discovered a live wire connected to Heidi's bathtub." Sensei repeated the message and gave George the phone.

"Where are you now?"

"Outside the big house on the lawn."

"Good. Get Tim or the old man to help you put Heidi in your passenger's seat. Buckle her up and go home to your house. You don't need to go back into the house. Stay outside. Did you tell Heidi not to use the phones in the house?"

"No. I didn't get a chance to tell her anything. When I got here the servants were crying and threatening to quit. It was bedlam. The chambermaid could have been electrocuted as well as Heidi. And the housekeeper says she almost pulled on the wire thinking that the kids had it plugged into a toy or something. She is still shaking. And everybody agrees that when somebody tries to kill Heidi, anyone in the way will also be killed."

"Don't mention my name, but go to the door and tell Heidi that everyone will be safe if she's not in the house. I have to be there on Saturday morning, so she has to be back by then. I don't want you inside the house. Are we clear about that?"

"Yes."

"Just take Heidi to your house now and get her back before Saturday morning... before 10 a.m. *Ciao*, Minx."

George looked at Sensei. "It's worse than I figured."

George purchased the garments he needed and returned to the office. He rehearsed his lines all the way back.

THURSDAY, NOVEMBER 3, 2011

Beryl believed that the best place to discover hard-to-find information was the mind of a good reference librarian. At the Media public library, she gained the attention of the librarian by going back and forth from a reference computer to the shelves and appearing to be frustrated in her mission to acquire information.

A tall blonde woman who announced herself as "Martha Myers, your reference librarian," asked Beryl if she needed a little assistance. Beryl supposed that she did.

"What are you trying to find?" Martha Myers asked.

"I'm ashamed to admit this but I've been hired to get as much background information on a suicide case, a young man's death that occurred about six or seven years ago, and I don't even know where to start."

"Do you know his name?"

"Yes. James Bielmann."

"Oh, yes. Tragic story. But all the articles about the incident have been transferred to microfiche. We've just installed a new system of accessing the information. I don't know how efficient it will prove to be in your case. Let me go and see just what the status is. I'll be right back."

Beryl checked the Periodical reference catalogue, looking up "Churches" with the sub-category of "Faith Healing." She got out her notebook and recorded several sources that appeared to be local.

Martha Myers looked over her shoulder. "Faith healing? Hmm. I don't think it would have helped the Bielmann boy. Poor kid."

"Is there much activity around here with faith-healing?" Beryl asked.

The librarian looked around and, finding no one who seemed to be in need of her assistance, indicated that she and Beryl should move to a more comfortable setting. In the corner of the room were stuffed chairs and a large coffee table. "Do you believe in faith healing?" she asked.

Beryl squinted. "I don't believe in it and I don't not believe in it. Frankly, so much of the evidence is anecdotal... not that this doesn't make it true. I definitely believe that there are psychosomatic problems that, being self-generated, are susceptible to self-cure."

"That's precisely how I feel," Ms. Myers said with the kind of surprised delight. "You can't dismiss the anecdotal accounts out of hand, but neither should you bet your life on them."

Sooner than she had expected, Beryl heard Ms. Myers say the name, "Michelson." She instructed her visitor, "Diane Michelson's case is the perfect 'case in point.' And, in fact, Mrs. Michelson has an oblique relationship to the Bielmann boy. There will be more detail in the files."

"I'd like to learn more about that relationship."

"Then why don't you come by tomorrow - I'll have the microfiche ready for you and then you can go down the block to the tea shop at about 12:30. We have our annual "Comicanza" charity event at the movie theater there. Old animated cartoons and amusing home videos transferred to film are shown. Friday is for the little children who don't go to school. Mrs. Michelson isn't likely to attend, but her husband Tim, who lives mostly out at the Bielmann place, will probably attend with their children. It starts at 1 p.m. The parking lot is across the street. He drives a big black Escalade."

"I will definitely be there."

Ms. Myers ended their conversation pleasantly. "I'll have them bring up the cassettes from 2004, that's when the suicide occurred. Or, if you want the whole family history for the last fifty years I can have all referent material sent, too. Do you have specific names?"

"I would really appreciate that," Beryl said. Lilyanne had obtained the vital statistics that Beryl needed. "Heidi and James Bielmann's mother was born in Denver, April 12, 1963. Her maiden name was Loman, Grace Eugenia Loman Bielmann. Their father is Hiram Danton Bielmann. He was born here in Media, Pennsylvania, on June 10th, 1961.

And, of course, Heidi... whose birthdate I don't have. I know she's about twenty-four years old."

"I'll pull up everything we have. See you tomorrow," Martha Myers said.

Beryl gave her a Wagner & Tilson business card and thanked her. This was the start of the biographical background.

George had purchased what he thought looked like an authentic Indian costume, a dark blue knee-length Nehru coat and white pants. He put the garments on and rehearsed his "bedside manner."

"You have a definite flair for acting," Beryl teased. "Try to recite your lines in front of a videocam so that posterity and I can savor the moment."

FRIDAY, NOVEMBER 4, 2011

It was noon before Sensei and Beryl reached the library. Instead of going in, they went down the street and parked in the lot near the movie theater. They went immediately to the tea shop next to the theater. Tables were set on the wide pavement. A sign informed them that outdoor service would end when the Comicanza ended. They ordered pumpkin pie and tea.

At twelve thirty, a black Escalade parked in the lot. Tim Michelson, holding the hands of his two children, walked across to the marquee.

"Mr. Michelson!" Beryl called.

Tim looked at them. "Are you calling me?"

"Yes... I can see that you're busy, but I won't take up much of your time. The movies are not due to start for another half hour."

"What is it that you want?" he smiled.

Beryl handed him her card. "I'm Beryl Tilson and this is Sensei Percy Wong, an associate of mine."

Tim glanced at the card. "Private Investigators?"

"Yes... we're looking into several accidents that may have been deliberate acts taken against Heidi Bielmann. We are interested in her interests, so to speak."

"Oh, Good," he said, sitting down after shaking hands with Sensei who immediately went to bring two chairs to the table for the children. "Are you working for an insurance company?"

Beryl acted as though he had correctly guessed her employer's identity. "I'm not at liberty to discuss my client. I'm so sorry. I wish I could be more..."

"That's fine. I understand completely. How can I help?"

"What we'd like is a little background information about life at Black Walnut Farm. Perhaps you know something about the accidents or the people who might want to hurt Heidi. In order to protect Heidi, we need to know from whom and from what. For example, we're sort of stuck right now with the sanitized version of James Bielmann's suicide. The newspapers print a version that suits their respective agendas. Can you give us a short but *true* account of that tragedy?"

"To do that story justice, we'd need a few weeks. But all right, the short version. Jimmy was the goofy looking son of two vain and attractive people. Heidi's odd looking, too; she's got a kind of large nose and bucked teeth, but I considered her my girl since we were kids. She's witty and good natured. It broke my heart when she went into a convent. But that's another story.

"Jimmy was skinny and that made him a target for bullying. For middle school, he was sent to a private boarding school here in town. The Bielmanns wouldn't get him on weekends, except for holidays when the school closed. Heidi got home on weekends because she got a ride home and back by one of the school's secretaries who passed the house.

"I remember when Jim was in 6th grade. The first Christmas that he was allowed to come home, he cried his heart out in my dad's arms. He was so lonely stuck in the dorm all weekend. So my dad tells him that in January, on a Saturday morning, he was to call home and say he needed a special book... or his prescription... or some sporting equipment - and my father would be sent to deliver it. He needed official permission to drive up to the kids' dormitories. The van had the Black Walnut Farm's logo painted on the door. My dad is the stable master of the estate, but I guess you already know that. Starting in January, Heidi and I would hide in the van and my dad would drive to school, sign in, and pick Jimmy up and we'd all go to the movies. Jimmy always saw a new movie before everybody else at school and that helped his ego. His braininess began to show. He was one smart kid.

"But then he went to prep school... to Corinth Academy, which was much farther away. He'd only be home on holidays. Same story. No friends. No invitations. And the price of gas started to climb and the

Bielmanns put an end to unnecessary travel. Jimmy was alone, but by nature, he was gregarious. He loved crowds and artistic displays. He had an interest in the theater arts - especially set design; and then, as he liked to tell it, one 'blessed day' he went into a hobby shop in a nearby town and met a girl who was stocking shelves. She was overweight and had bad skin, but she was sweet and innocent. She was also crazy about set design. She showed him some dioramas - shoe boxes decorated inside like a theater stage. She had won a prize for her imaginary production of *Hamlet*. He flipped out. Here was a kindred spirit. Every chance they got they would create scenery for various dramas. I guess it's not as weird as it might seem. Evidently a lot of research and skill are needed, plus a knowledge of the play. Anyway, that's what Jimmy lived for. And he was in love the way only teenagers can be in love.

"He asked my father for advice. He wanted to bring her home for Thanksgiving Dinner. Should he invite her? To my father's everlasting regret, he told him it was a wonderful idea and he advised him to ask his parents for permission to invite her. Jimmy asked if he could invite a 'fellow set design fanatic' to the dinner. They said he could. My dad and Jim drove out to pick up Louise - that was her name - at her home. Louise came from a poor family, like eight people living in a house trailer. My dad and Jim went inside to meet her parents and the rest of the family - who were apparently big drinkers, and then they came back here. My father blames himself. He actually cries when he talks about this. Louise wore her best dress which happened to be a summer dress and Louise didn't know how to hold her knife and fork. The Bielmanns saw how lovingly he looked at her, and they were furious and didn't bother to conceal it.

"At dinner, they were vicious and insulted Louise about her weight, her dress, her table manners, her poverty. And Hiram topped it off by chastising James. 'A gentleman does not bring a female of this type home to his parents' table.' Jimmy stood up - Heidi told this to me - and told them how he hated them, how all they ever worried about was superficial shit; and they came right back at him telling him how looking at him over a dinner table was disgusting enough - without him bringing a pus-faced creature like Louise with him.

"Louise runs out of the house and James goes to ask my father to drive him and Louise to her house. They get in the car and drive after her, but she makes it to the highway ahead of them and gets picked up by someone.

"She never went home, but she did check in with her mother. She said she was getting a job with a theater production company, and she'd have a permanent address soon. So, no missing person's report was ever filed.

"At first, Jimmy didn't know where to look. During Christmas vacation he went to her house and that's when he saw the postcard she had sent from New York. In January he went up to New York - against the Bielmanns' orders - and started making the rounds of the set design companies in New York. And in February, he went again. Nothing. He went up there again in March. Twice. In April, he went again and this time he checked with the police and somebody let him look through a book of photographs of unidentified adolescent bodies. He saw Louise's morgue photo. Two weeks after that Thanksgiving dinner, she jumped off a bridge and drowned. James took down the location and the number of her grave marker. He went to the cemetery, curled up over the marker, and slit his wrists. He bled out. End of story."

"And that's when Heidi decided to go into the convent?" Sensei asked.

"Yes. The event ended Jimmy's life; and it changed ours forever. You have to appreciate how close we were. We were happy as kids. We'd play adventure games. Jungle dwellers! I remember how we shaved and striped one of their white poodles to be our pet tiger. We used a permanent marker. The damned dog looked like a clown for years. All those days were gone. We weren't kids anymore. Heidi grieved. I grieved. She prayed for James' soul because he committed suicide. She was a Catholic. I am, too. But I figured he had been murdered by them. It was easy for me. They weren't my bloody relatives. From that day on, my father hated them with a passion. He would repeat, 'Why did I believe that they'd be happy to see him so happy? I should have warned him, instead.' Who could have foreseen that kind of cruelty?"

"Where is he buried?" Beryl asked.

"No place. They had him cremated and put inside an urn which they put in the attic. And yes... in case you're wondering, my dad paid to have Louise exhumed and her body to be brought down here and cremated. Her family didn't seem to care. Where can you store an urn inside a house trailer with two adults who drink and five kids? When they didn't pick up the ashes at the mortician's office, my dad asked them if they would mind if he got them. He got them and yes... he mixed their ashes. I thought my dad was going to have a heart attack or a nervous breakdown. He felt so guilty."

"What about Hiram and Loreen? Are they the perfect couple that they pretend to be?" Beryl asked.

"Hell, no. He had many women in town. One time Loreen rented a car so that he wouldn't recognize it and spied on him when he went to his club. A blonde pulls up to the entrance and Hiram comes out and gets into the passenger side and kisses her. Loreen takes photographs and gets the license number; and then she tries to blackmail the woman who happened to be married. The gal wouldn't pay so Loreen got her revenge and caused a scandal. The husband beat the woman senseless and went to jail for two years. But it didn't stop Hiram. A few months later he had a new blonde."

Beryl shook her head. "We understand that the Bielmann family is local. Did you know them?"

"I knew who they were, that's all. They were upper class, but poor. They lost all their money in the Savings and Loan scandals back in the 'eighties... that was after Grace married him. Mrs. Bielmann - the former Grace Loman - then had all the money. Loreen's family had neither money nor social standing."

The children were getting restless. As Tim stood up, Beryl asked, "Can you answer one quick question? What can you tell us about that riding accident that Heidi had a few months ago?"

"That was no accident. Somebody had strung a cord across the bridal path... high up... so that it hit the rider, not the horse. The cord broke when Heidi hit it, but it knocked her out of the saddle. It could have broken her neck. As it was, she was dragged thirty yards or so. She never filed a police report or an insurance claim."

"We know that her use of a wheelchair is just a cover for her to be able to keep you living at Black Walnut. How is that working out?"

"Ah, so you know. It's amazing that she wasn't hurt that bad. I took her down to Baltimore and had her checked out. She lets everybody think she was hurt in the accident. I went out and looked in the scene of the accident. The cord was gone but I found the marks it left on the tree trunks on either side of the path. She's trying to get her father and his wife and her kids out of the house. Eviction ain't a simple matter."

"Does Loreen Bielmann ride?"

"Yes. I taught her, myself. Hiram also rides. In fact, he's quite the equestrian. Dressage and all that."

The children had gotten up and were tugging at Tim's sleeves. "It's time to go," Tim said, shaking hands with Sensei and nodding to Beryl.

Beryl and Sensei went directly to the librarian's desk. Miss Myers was disappointed. "They don't have the reference material ready yet," she apologized. "Can you come back tomorrow morning? We close at noon."

"I'll be here," Beryl said. "Count on it."

SATURDAY, NOVEMBER 5, 2011

George, wearing an 'achkan' Nehru coat, tight white pants, and long white shirt, sat upright in Beryl's car contemplating his next move.

Although he knew his lines, he still experienced a twinge of stage-fright. Sensei, with Beryl's help had pomaded and sprayed his naturally wavy hair until it lay straight back on his head like a skullcap. He looked older and wiser, but he felt like a fool. "Jesus," he said, as he opened the car door and glanced in the side-view mirror, "I look stupid. Too late for Halloween."

Beryl reached into the back seat of her Bronco. "No, it's not. Here!" She produced a large paper bag. "It isn't black and orange, but what the hell. Do you realize you'll be the first person in Christendom who dressed up like Nehru for Halloween? Just keep that Indian lilt in your voice when you say, 'Trrrick or Trrreat.'"

George looked at her. "Are there circumstances in which it is permissible to punch a woman's lights out?"

"No. Not even in self-defense. Ok. I'll work on my Indian accent." She began to sing, "Trrick or Trrree-eat."

George remained in the passenger's seat. He took the bag and opened it, and in one swift move, pulled it down over Beryl's head. "Now you're the Unknown Detective."

She did not remove the bag and when he looked around after ringing the doorbell and saw her sitting there with the bag covering her head, he began to laugh. He had to turn his back to the houseboy who opened the door.

"Yes?" the boy said. "May I help you?"

George rubbed his eyes. He suppressed the urge to laugh aloud and turned around, cleared his throat, and answered, "I'd like to see Miss Bielmann." His accent could not have belonged to any known country.

"Is she expecting you?"

"No. I'm afraid not. I'm on a mission of mercy." He cringed, thinking that he sounded as though he were under water; but his tone conveyed such determination that the houseboy decided he might as well keep the flies out of the house by letting him in.

George looked around the foyer. At one side of the large room was a portrait of a handsome young couple. A plaque beside the painting said that it was of Hiram Bielmann and his late former wife, Grace Loman Bielmann. Grace, George thought, looked and dressed a lot like Imelda Marcos.

"Do you have a card?" the boy asked.

"No. I'm afraid not. I've gotten to the point in life that mandates that one's reputation should precede one, and that if it does not, more than a card can follow it." He asked himself what the hell he meant by that, but he could not answer his question.

Hiram Bielmann came into the foyer and rescued him from self-doubt. "Who are you? Or perhaps I should say, what are you?"

"I am a faith-healer. My name is Swami Swahananda. I am not looking for money. In fact, I will accept no money. I seek only the opportunity to assist Miss Bielmann in her medical distress."

Bielmann knew his lines and called for his wife. "Loreen! Honey! You've gotta come here and see this for yourself. Another quack is at our door."

Heidi rolled into the foyer in a wicker wheelchair. "*Our* door? No, Daddy. Another quack is at *my* door."

It offended George that she had elected to correct only the possessive adjective. Regardless of whose door it was, he, evidently, was still a quack. "Ah, Miss Bielmann, I believe?"

"And you must be the famous faith-healer who though born and raised in Milwaukee, Wisconsin was trained by the world-renowned

Guru Swamiji Krishnapurti in all the ancient Vedic arts of healing that were given to the world during the time of the Raj."

George cringed, faking a smile and wondering why the hell with all her money she hadn't spent a few bucks on acting lessons. He pressed his palms together and said, "I am at your service."

Heidi was indeed a rather homely girl with front teeth that slanted outwards and trailed lines of saliva when she spoke. She wore glasses through which she squinted, and her nose, as reported, was unfortunately large.

"I am honored to have you call upon me, Swami. Would you like to examine my back before you attempt to heal me with faith?"

"Ah, that would be most desirable, Miss Bielmann. But I don't want to make you uncomfortable in any way."

"My houseboy, Angus, will carry me upstairs. I have a downstairs wheelchair and an upstairs wheelchair. I have had many strangers examine my back. I am used to it. It is for a good cause and I am safe here at home. Please follow us." The houseboy picked her up and carried her up the stairs, depositing her in the waiting wheelchair. "Both of my regular chairs," she said, "are in the repair shop." She looked up at him as though she expected him to comment.

"Alas!" George mumbled. "I have no power to heal chairs." He cursed himself for this inanity.

George checked the hallway as he wheeled her into her bedroom. There was a new light fixture on the wall. He recognized it from catalog photos. It concealed two stationary motion detection cameras that would have completely covered the hall.

Heidi kept to the script and asked him to examine her spine. He glanced around the room as she discussed her "vertebras" and spinal cord. He could not see any surveillance device; but he imagined that if there were one, it would be inside the smoke detector or wall lamp. "I believe that I have seen enough of your problem. I also believe that it will yield to divine intervention." He helped her into her upstairs wheelchair and pushed it to where she parked it near the top of the stairs. The houseboy came up the stairs and carried Heidi down, putting her into her downstairs wheelchair.

"Let us go out into the garden, Swami Swahananda," she said. "It is a beautiful day. It is much too beautiful outside to spend the day inside. Do you not agree?"

"Yes," George agreed. "A capital idea." He went to her wheelchair and began to push it. "Allow me," he said.

"Pay no attention to these people," Heidi enunciated clearly, gesturing towards Hiram and Loreen. "They have delusions of grandeur." Looking heavenward, George pushed her out the front door and lowered her wheelchair down the ramp that led to a sidewalk.

Heidi directed him. "Straight ahead and then at the corner, turn left. That is where we will find the garden."

In the garden, amid huge clusters of chrysanthemums, George whispered in her ear, "I'm going to carry you over to one of the benches and you can tell me the latest news." He picked her up and placed her on the wrought iron bench.

"Nothing much to tell. On Wednesday morning the servants found a hot wire that had been threaded through the plumbing into my bathtub. I know that I have to do something to stop them, but I simply don't know what to do. I got home yesterday from Lily's house. God knows what they did while I was gone. I used to have two battery-powered wheelchairs - one downstairs and one upstairs. You know that I can walk perfectly well, but then I'd lose the excuse to have Tim stay with me. A few weeks ago my downstairs one wouldn't run. My father took down an old wicker chair we had in the attic. And then a few days ago my other wheelchair wouldn't run so my father took it to the repair shop and brought this wicker wheelchair home. Then things started to happen to the old chair... the wheel fell off. Every day there's another accident. And if I say something it becomes proof that I'm crazy. I need to prove that they're doing these things. I can't complain to the police. They'll find out for certain that I can walk and they'll also make life miserable for Tim and his family."

George went to the chair and looked at the wheel mounting. "It wouldn't be hard to sabotage. Jesus. A cotter pin! That's all it's got. What does Tim say about it?"

"He's been after me to get private investigators in here to help us. I talked to Lilyanne and she directed me to you. She adores you. And I trust Lily."

"Why can't you just evict them?" George asked.

"My father filed his own suit, claiming my mother forged his signature on documents that conveyed to her his interests in the house and all its appurtenances. Plus, they've threatened to scandalize Tim and me. It would devastate his wife. I'm sure she knows about us, but it's private knowledge.

"They hate it that Tim's father is living in the house. The carriage house is uninhabitable. While I was in the convent, a septic tank backed up and sewage flowed into the basement. Mice, roaches, ants. No air conditioning... and the stench. He had bites all over him. He coughs and his joints ache. I insisted that he move into the main house immediately - on the second floor because he was too weak to keep climbing to the servants' rooms on the third.

"That I've let a servant live upstairs is more proof of my incompetence. So Tim said he loved me and whether he does or doesn't, he stays with me in my bed, and I like having him there. There's something that's not entirely genuine about our relationship, but it's not a malevolent thing. His wife rejected him. I appreciate him. She's happy only with the people from her church. I offered to pay for a kidney transplant, but she declined. She really believes that faith healing baloney."

"If she knows about you and Tim, she may not want to accept your help. If the money came from another source, she might take it. By now she must know that she's not getting better despite all the praying."

"I tried that. I tried to get the transplant surgeon to accept the money as an anonymous gift, but she still refused."

"Doesn't she realize that she'll die without a transplant?"

"I keep having to remember that her illness may be clouding her judgment. Also I don't think her crazy pride will let her admit that she's been wrong about that church. That pride will kill her."

"Will you and Tim get married then?"

"No. For the sake of the kids, we'd have to wait. The kids will have to live with our decision. You know how people talk. If we don't wait, they'll remind the kids for the rest of their lives that their mother wasn't even cold in her grave before their father remarried. Someday, maybe."

George nodded. "Who takes care of her now?"

"I gave $50,000 to her faith-healing church to hire a few members of the flock to live in the house with her and give her care around the clock, five days a week. I replenish the fund."

"And the kids?"

"They're mostly here. Tim takes them to nursery school every day. Weekends and one day a week, they're at his home in Media."

"Your father thinks you bought his wife's house to spite him. Why did you buy it?"

"The house was foreclosed on. I hoped that if I bought it I could give it to my father and get them out of here. But they weren't interested. Then I thought since it was bigger than Tim's current house, the people who were helping his wife would have better accommodations in it. But Tim's wife refused to move."

"You're in danger here. You need proof that they're trying to hurt you. Meanwhile, they're trying to get evidence on you that will help them to get you committed for psychiatric problems. When was that hallway lamp installed?"

"Just this week."

"I know the equipment. There are two fixed motion-sensitive cameras in it. No sound. I don't know what other surveillance equipment they've installed. I told them that it would be a very expensive proposition so I guess they shopped around until they found somebody who would do it cheaply. Do you own the house completely?"

"Yes."

"An ethical installer wouldn't bug a non-owner's home. Maybe they lied to him or maybe he wasn't ethical. But you have the right to install whatever you want in your own home, especially in light of the attempts made on your life. This is what I propose: let me hire electronic surveillance experts. You have to keep everyone out of the house for a few hours. They'll plant cameras and bugs. The units will have to be monitored on site since you don't have any wireless capability. We can use a bedroom closet. When is the earliest you can get everyone out?"

Heidi thought for a moment. "Tuesday is Election Day! November 8th. They'll go into town to vote."

"Good! What about the servants and Tim and his father?"

"Lilyanne told me not to tell Tim about any of this. I can tell them that I failed to register to vote and that I feel terrible that this house isn't upholding its civic duty. I'll give the servants the day off. Tim can take them and his father into town, and I can get him to go to an architect's office to see about designing new stables and a carriage house. I'll insist that my father and Loreen be there, too."

"That will work. Ok. The installers will need to know whether or not there are any other cameras on site. You don't want somebody else's cameras recording your team as they install your cameras. So I'll bring you a sweeping device for you to locate any cameras and bugs. Keep your bedroom door locked. Make sure the foyer's clear of devices before you let the men in. Do you have a dog on the property?"

"Yes, two of them. Boxers."

"We'll have to neutralize them. Can you give them shots to put them to sleep for a few hours."

"Yes. I'm not a city girl."

"I'll get two syringes to you before the installers come. I'll put them beside the front door. I'll leave the sweeping device there, too. If you need help with it, my guy will give you instructions outside the house. How many bedrooms do you have in the main house?"

"On the second floor, nine. There are four bedrooms on either side of the hallway, and then, there's a door where the hallway ends. That door is to the master's bedroom - which is as wide as the entire floor. My father and Loreen use that room. On the third floor there are two storage rooms and eight bedrooms - for the servants and extra guests."

"Big place," George said.

"The rooms are on the small side. When the house was built there were no cars to take visitors home. When people came, they stayed a few days. And if the weather was bad, that could turn into weeks."

"Our office is old, too. Pre-electricity. All right. When I leave now, call an architect and make sure that the appointment is on Tuesday around noon. If Tim's kids don't have day school on Election Day, tell him to take them to their mother's house. When the house is empty and the dogs are asleep just open the front door and sit in the doorway. That will signal the installers. If somebody reports seeing strange men, say that you saw mice and called an exterminator, and that's who the strange men were. Their van has an exterminator's logo on the side."

"Can Lilyanne come here on Tuesday? I'd really like that."

George laughed. "No... no one is to know about it. She might innocently say something."

George wheeled Heidi back into the house. "Now you be sure to do your meditation routine faithfully. Faith healing requires faith. That is the most important thing for you to remember."

Beryl was eager to drive into town. She had taken the bag off her head and, from the parking area, had seen George wheel Heidi down to the garden.

George was glad to have finished his performance. "Let's go home."

"I promised the librarian I'd be there before noon. We've got exactly one hour to get there and get the copies of the articles she dug out for me."

They drove directly to the Media public library, and while George waited in the car, Beryl rushed in to keep her appointment.

"I was afraid that I had gathered all this material for nothing," Martha Myers admonished Beryl. She indicated the stack of microfiche cassettes. "They must be returned to their proper niches before I lock the door - and we close at noon."

Beryl apologized. "My lateness is inexcusable. Clearly, there's no way I can do this work by noon. Is there anyone around who can do the job?" Beryl took two five-hundred dollar bills from the 'mad money' slot in her purse. "I don't intend to get paid for work that someone else does.

So here's a thousand dollars. Can someone on your staff do it on his or her own time?"

Miss Myers protested. "It is too much! The job is so automated now... really. There is not that much to be done."

"If you are willing to do it, wonderful. If you want to hire someone else, fine. Can you scan the articles and email them to me?"

"The new equipment does everything automatically. It directs the machine to every article in which the Bielmann name is mentioned. And then I just put in your email address hit "email" and you've got it. It's really not worth a thousand dollars."

"To me, it is. You've been a Godsend, Martha Myers."

"What specifically are you looking for?"

"Just family history."

"Grace Loman Bielmann was from Denver, Colorado. We won't find much history on her in this library. She came to the area in the 80's. Now Hiram Bielmann? Yes. There's more written about him and his family. And his son's suicide was covered at great length."

"If you give me your cell and email number," Beryl said, "I'll try to find out where Grace Loman Bielmann went to school in Denver. Maybe there's a way you can tap into those files."

"I'll try. Sometimes it is all electronically done. You don't even have to deal with another human being. I'll send you everything as quickly as I can."

Beryl extended her hand. As they shook hands the librarian said, "There's one peculiar thing I came across that I thought you might be interested in."

"Yes?"

"I found photographs of Hiram Bielmann from when he was a boy. He won some kind of chess tournament. I've never seen such a radical change in appearance. He's a handsome man now... but then! Oooh. He was nothing to write home about, if you know what I mean."

"That interests me. Do you happen to know where he went to school as a boy?"

"Yes. He went to Valmont. It's a private preparatory school."

"Valmont? I always thought a son went to his father's school," Beryl said. "James went to Corinth Academy."

"That's curious. I wonder why. Well, we need more information. Be sure to get me the name of Grace Loman's school."

"I will," Beryl assured her. "I will definitely do that. Thank you so much. You may have earned your salary already."

"Were you too late?" George asked as Beryl returned to the car.

"Not too late at all," Beryl replied. "We may be onto something. We need to find out where Heidi's mother went to school... prep and college. And you said that Hiram had a beard. Describe it."

"One of those professorial beards... less than an inch long... trimmed nicely."

Beryl pulled out into traffic. George took out his cellphone and called Lily's cellphone.

Lily answered. "I see I am being called by a beast. My beast."

George responded in a voice that made Beryl roll her eyes. "How am I supposed to respond to that? Like that old Cuban dictator, 'I may be a beast, but I'm *your* beast.' Is that it?"

"Ask her!" Beryl insisted.

"Beryl wants to know where Grace Loman Bielmann went to school... prep and college. Call me back at the office or my house. I hate these damned cell things."

"Where are you now?" Lily asked.

"We're just leaving the Media public library."

"Come by here for lunch!"

George turned to Beryl. "Do you want to go out to Tarleton House for lunch."

"No. We have too much work to do. But thank her anyway. Another time, definitely."

George, annoyed that Beryl had rejected the invitation so quickly, expressed his regrets and ended the call.

"Are you pouting?" Beryl asked.

"You could have thought about it a little more before you said, 'no.'"

"What is there to think about? Have you forgotten how you're dressed? An hour ago you felt ridiculous in your swami outfit. But... by all means... if you want to be seen with your hair glued down, let's stop and show young Lilyanne Smith how old you can look when you try."

"You are a nag. A buzz-kill. Let's just go home."

They parked in the rear of their office building and climbed the back stairs up to the second floor's kitchen door of Beryl's apartment. George showered to get the 'gook' out of his hair and changed back into his 'secular' jeans and sweater.

Beryl made lunch. "Get it while it's hot!"

"I'm hungry." George came to the table and groaned as he saw the "green goddess on pita bread" sandwich. "Can't you ever serve real food?"

"Yes, but not to middle aged men who think they're seventeen. I also have cantaloupe."

The phone rang. The office phone had an extension in Beryl's "all purpose" office/bedroom. George sat on her bed and answered it.

Lilyanne's voice said, "Beast! Tell Beryl that Heidi's mother went to Carrington Honors in Denver... a prep school. For college she went to the University of Nevada, Reno."

Beryl came into the room to see a concerned look on George's face. "Gee," he said weakly, "You got that information fast."

"Anything for my very own beast. I asked and she answered right away."

Beryl went to the phone. "Is that Lily?"

George nodded. "Lily... just a minute." He looked up at Beryl. "She called Heidi and asked her where her mother went to school."

"Damn," Beryl whispered. "Now what?" she sighed. "Well, don't scare her. Ask her where Heidi went to school."

"Lily, where did Heidi go to school?"

"She never went to college but she did go to Prep School. Burgess in Swarthmore."

"You are the most wonderful creature God ever made. But don't quote me."

"Tell Beryl that Jack and Groff are meeting Margaret Cioran and me for a skiing holiday over Christmas. Jack wants to clear it with her in case she made plans. It's Margaret's first "outing" since the disaster."

He relayed the message to Beryl and then hung up, looking forlorn. "What the hell is wrong with me? I forgot to tell her not to ask Heidi on the phone. I didn't specify that this information had something to do with the investigation. I was joking about that beast thing. I just said you wanted to know. They are not stupid people. If they're bugging that phone, they'll figure it out."

"She may have asked in the course of a normal conversation. Don't push it. Get your electronic surveillance guy on the phone and let's get moving with the case. I'll make tea. Here..." she flicked through her iPhone. "Jeff Gable's private line." She handed him the phone.

At two o'clock the librarian started to transmit via email copies of microfiche articles. Beryl let them all come in before she assigned them to "Print." The published accounts were slanted in favor of guilt-free parental involvement. Louise was not mentioned. Instead, a mental affliction of unknown origin had plagued the boy and in a serious bout of depression, he killed himself. None of the reported facts jibed with the information they had obtained from Tim.

George, needing to verify Tim's version, called a contact in the Medical Examiner's office. He gave the name and date and waited for a call-back which came in a few minutes.

"On April 11, 2005, the Bielmann kid slashed his wrists at the gravesite of an unidentified teenager, #F8917, who was later identified as Louise Pulaski, a runaway. For him the box 'exsanguination' is checked. I looked up her report which says that a dental review indicated that she was about sixteen years of age. She had been found in the East River on December 8th, 2004, a drowning victim, an apparent suicide. The coroner estimated that she had been in the water three days. Her clothing was size 15. That's a girl's measurement. Ladies use even numbers - or so my wife tells me. No jewelry. The body was exhumed and returned to Pennsylvania, *et cetera. et cetera.* You need any more?"

"No," said George. "It would seem like a Romeo and Juliet story."

"Yeah... Romeo and Juliet. Can't get away from Shakespeare, can ya'. Kids."

SUNDAY, NOVEMBER 6, 2011

George would usually stay home on Sunday and watch football. On this Sunday, he went to the office instead and did background checks on Timothy Michelson, Hiram Bielmann and Loreen Murray Jessup Bielmann. His contact at the police department told him that Tim and Loreen had "clean sheets" but Hiram had a few problems: domestic squabbles and fights over failure to pay debts.

He could hear Beryl upstairs, moving furniture. He wondered if he should go up and help her. Maybe she didn't want company. Maybe he didn't feel like talking to anyone. George recognized his restless malaise. It came every year around the holidays. Maybe it had something to do with "case-anxiety," but mostly it was simply that he missed his children who were growing up without him in California. Then, too, Lilyanne Smith was going skiing with Beryl's son Jack and another couple. The Young Professionals shushing down the slopes... singing and knowing all the words to songs he never even heard of. He needed to toughen himself for the holidays. He was becoming too sensitive.

He decided to make life easier for everyone and go home to watch the West Coast games.

At home, he parked in his driveway and held onto the steering wheel. Bending over it he murmured, "My life has turned to shit." Fifteen minutes passed before he entered his house.

MONDAY, NOVEMBER 7, 2011

After working for hours consulting with physicians and organizing the Bielmann's files, Beryl called George and Sensei and asked them to come by after Monday night's services. She had not seen George since Saturday.

"First," she said as they pulled their chairs around the little kitchen table, "some background on Tim Michelson. He's twenty-six, married to a woman who has an incurable kidney disease. George checked and he's had no arrests."

She produced several photographs of Tim. "As you can see, he's not so handsome now, but he used to be. His father is a lifetime stableman at Black Walnut Farm. Tim became a blacksmith's apprentice. Between the forge, the anvil, and the actual shoeing of horses, he received more than his share of injuries. He got kicked in the face a few times, and he has had a lot of little burns. He was offered a job as a farrier at the Garden State Race Track, but he didn't want to leave his wife and kids and his father. Heidi was in the convent at the time. Finally he settled on being an assistant to his father and giving riding lessons in town Let's move on.

"In one of the articles the librarian sent me, it mentioned that James Bielmann, Heidi's brother, attended Corinth Academy at the time of his death. Usually the son goes to school where the father went. Martha Myers, the Media Librarian, confirmed that Hiram Bielmann attended Valmont Prep. We also learned that while Heidi went to New Burgess Girls' Preparatory, her mother attended Carrington Honors in Denver. This seemed strange so I looked into it.

"Both parents went to these prep schools for four years and that meant they had a photograph taken every year for the year book. These prep schools will sell you digital copies of pages or articles from any year book. Give them your credit card number and into your Mac comes the picture or article you want. The librarian ordered all four photos and the captions, for each of Heidi's parents. As to Hiram Bielmann, George recently met the man in person." She opened a folder and removed four photographs. "Does this look like a young Hiram Bielmann?"

The yearbook photographs were of a remarkably homely teen aged boy. His nose was prominent and arched. His chin seemed to recede into his Adams Apple. His ears were completely perpendicular to his nose. "It can't be!" George said, amazed at the transformation.

"Yes," said Beryl, "it is. We've all heard about these nose jobs and ear jobs... but I got technical advice. I talked to a plastic surgeon. They don't do cosmetic surgery on kids. A teenager has to stop his growth phase before they'll do any remodeling. Rhinoplasty is the surgical procedure that transforms a nose. They'll straighten it if it's crooked, enlarge it if it's small, and chisel it down if it's big. But until the kid is old enough, he can go around with a schnoz like a toucan and they won't touch it.

"Otoplasty is what they call ear flattening surgery. The surgeon actually goes behind the ear and removes a lot of stuff and sews the ear back flat. Again, this is after the kid stops growing.

"Orthognathic surgery will give you a new mandible... a jaw like Michael Douglas's if that's what you want. So Hiram's family had enough money at the time to get his face beautified. These procedures would have cost thousands... many thousands.

"But, here's the problem. They can change the face, but they can't change the genes that made the face. Which may be why he was so eager to adopt Loreen's kids. They're good looking from the few photos I saw of them. Maybe he wanted them to have his last name. But let's hold that in abeyance... and move on to the lady that George said reminded him of Imelda Marcos in her portrait.

"Look at the beautiful Grace Loman as a teenager." Beryl produced four photographs of Grace. "If I sound cruel," Beryl prefaced her remarks, "it's because I remember what she did to that poor girl Louise. I'm angry about that. I admit it. I'm angry about that Thanksgiving dinner. The two of them should have been horsewhipped. It was inexcusable. In the first photograph Grace must have been too young for braces and her teeth lifted her upper lip until, as you can see, it looks like an awning. She has braces in the subsequent photos but she also has pimples... so many that her face looks like medium velocity blood splatter. Personally, I can't imagine *her* parents letting her skin go untreated to this extent. It's criminal negligence."

"This is the woman in that portrait?" George asked incredulously. "Unbelievable!"

"Would those pimples leave pocked skin?" Beryl asked rhetorically. "Of course they would. But L.S.R. - Laser Skin Resurfacing - takes care of that. So orthodontics for the teeth and chemical peels or laser resurfacing for the skin. Throw in some breast augmentation and you've got a beauty queen. A very pretty woman. Unfortunately, nothing changes the genes that caused the problem teeth and skin."

Sensei laughed. "So Hiram and Grace meet, and each thinks the other is beautiful or handsome. They marry and have two kids who are as homely as they were in their now-camouflaged pasts. That's karma."

Beryl nodded. "Then came tragedy with James and Louise, and Heidi's decision to enter the convent. Grace and Hiram divorce. Grace learns that she's got lung cancer.

"Black Walnut Farm was given to them by Grace's family as a wedding present. Her father lived in the house for many years. She gave Hiram millions for his half and then he refused to leave the house. He files a countersuit and privately threatens to create a scandal that will destroy Tim's family. Almost everything is routine greed and dysfunctional family crap. What they did to Louise and James and currently to Heidi is outrageous. Those kids had two vipers for parents."

"Geez," said Sensei. "It makes my own childhood seem normal."

"Poor kids," George said. "Probably every insult that had been hurled at Hiram and Grace, they hurled at their own kids. Why would they do that when they know how it feels?"

Sensei answered. "It's because they suffered their disfigurements as kids. When adults sustain a crippling injury or deformity, they retain their old self-image and even if they're embarrassed about it, their respectful attitude towards other people is already formed. They haven't been warped by hurtful comments made by onlookers. But so often you find that people who have been distressed as kids, can turn out to be overly emotional and defensive. They can be friendly to a few people and downright nasty to a multitude. Something happens to their ability to empathize. That's why bullying little kids is such a crime, abusing them and ridiculing them for any sub-standard feature. No charge for the lecture."

TUESDAY, NOVEMBER 8, 2011

Tuesday morning at 9:30 a.m., George positioned himself on a nearby hill and with his binoculars watched Black Walnut Farm. Half an hour later, he saw Jeff Gable's 'Exterminator' truck park at the side of the road. Jeff Gable used a two-way radio phone to communicate with George. Everything so far was on schedule for the 10 a.m. surveillance installation. Unfortunately, Hiram Bielmann's Mercedes did not come down the driveway until 11 a.m. George's "walkie-talkie" rang.

"You said the Mercedes would pass with the client's father and step-mother in it," Gable announced. "He just drove past us. He's alone."

"Jesus," George said. "Heidi said that they often pulled this... pretended to go out and then stayed behind to spy on her. We'll have to wait it out. Maybe she'll be leaving in her own car."

It was eleven-thirty before Tim's Escalade left. George called Jeff Gable. "They have a noon appointment with the architect. I can't imagine that Loreen would be absent from that meeting. We'll just have to continue to wait."

"It's gonna cost her for our time," Jeff warned.

"She knows that. But what's she gonna do? She can't drug the dogs until the house is empty."

At 12:20 p.m. Loreen finally left the house. George immediately drove down to the front door and put the syringes and the detection device in a bag on a ledge behind a bush near the front door. He could hear the dogs barking.

Before he had driven off the property, the front door opened and Heidi came out in her wicker wheelchair and picked up the bag.

By 1 p.m. she still had not appeared in the doorway to signal them that the dogs were asleep and the downstairs had been swept.

Finally at 1:15 she did appear in the doorway, and the Exterminator's van pulled into Black Walnut Farm's drive and circled to the far side of the house. George watched with his binoculars as Jeff approached Heidi. She, Jeff, and three of his men entered the house.

Five minutes later, Hiram Bielmann's Mercedes pulled into the drive. George called Jeff's phone to warn him. Loreen's car was less than half a mile behind Hiram's. Heidi appeared in the doorway and, George supposed, Jeff Gable and his crew went out a rear exit and got in the van. After the Bielmanns entered the front of the house, the van came around from the rear and drove to the highway. Jeff called to tell George that the mission had to be aborted.

It was late and George was hungry. He called Beryl and told her to tell Sensei that he was going to pick up three Caesar's salads and Italian bread at a Deli Sensei liked.

The tea kettle simmered as George arrived with the salads and Sensei set the table. Beryl kept out the Bielmann file to record George's notes on the morning's surveillance.

After they had finished eating, they resumed discussing the case. "Does Heidi know any of this prep school photo business?" George asked.

"That," said Beryl, "I don't know."

George had left the back door unlocked when he returned with the Deli food. Without anyone's notice, Lilyanne Smith had opened the door and entered the kitchen. "Does Heidi know what about prep school photos and what is it that the omniscient Beryl Tilson doesn't know?" She did not wait for an answer. She crossed the room in a few strides and hurled herself onto George's lap. She wrapped her arms around his neck and began kissing his face and head. "My beast! My wonderful beast!"

"Oh my God," George groaned and struggled to get up. "Stop that! And what are you doing here?"

"Mohammed would not go to the mountain, so the mountain went to Mohammed. What is so strange about a newly licensed driver coming here?"

"This is a place of business! I don't hear from you for months and next thing you're my new room mate. This is a business conference!"

"What business requires all that garlic? Are you professional vampire busters? Oh yes... I can see and even smell all that garlic from what..." she looked in the sink, "Caesar's salad?"

Lilyanne flipped open the file folder and saw Hiram's boyhood photo. "Ugh!" she said, "Are these the Bielmanns?"

George pushed her off his lap, stood up, and brought a stool to the table. "Sit down, Minx." She did not sit.

"If you're wondering whether Heidi has seen photos of how her parents used to look, the answer is yes. She saw her mother's picture when she visited Denver. And then everybody who is anybody in a fifty mile radius of Black Walnut Farm knows what Hiram looked like as a kid. My father says that all that plastic surgery never improved his personality or his character. He evidently borrows things he doesn't return... money, mostly."

"When did Heidi tell you she knew about her parents' surgical history?" Sensei asked.

"In the convent. We have no secrets in the convent."

"Does the Minx want tea?" George asked.

Lily looked at Beryl as she held George's face. "Does this dreadful creature know how beautifully blue his eyes are... with their dark lashes... in this blue shirt? Who bought him this blue shirt? It's heavenly! And no, the Minx does not want tea. The Minx has to go and vote for the first time in her life... and she will be driving the new white Jaguar her father gave her. She will drive - all by herself - to the polls in a somewhat distant county."

"I'm notifying the Highway Department," George said sternly. "They need to be on the lookout for a white Jaguar with a crazed minx at the wheel. *Thirty-Three-Sixty-Two. Approach with caution. Minx is Armed and Dangerous.*"

"I told you all that he was a beast. Now do you believe me?" Lily turned up her face and stepped closer to him. "Quick quick slow. Quick quick slow. When are you going to teach me to dance again?"

"When hell freezes over or the sun becomes a red giant... whichever comes first."

"Lighten up on the garlic," she said. "Or else include me in your invitation list."

Sensei and Beryl merely looked at each other and said nothing.

The office phone rang. "Thank God," said George. "I'm going to answer it. Go... with God."

"Isn't he wonderful?" Lilyanne whispered. Then, as she left by the back door, she called, "I'll show you my car another time!"

Jeff Gable called to discuss the next opportunity to attempt an installation.

"I need to talk to the client," George said. "And the phones are probably bugged. So I'll have to let you know about that. Did you learn anything out there?"

"One of my men located the monitor of the hall lamp camera system. It was locked in a china cabinet in the dining room which is right under the hall lamp fixture on the floor above."

"Did you recognize whose work it was... the other installation?" George asked.

"Yes... a start-up outfit from Philly. "C.S.I. which stands for Complete Surveillance Installations. And there are only two cameras on the second floor. The client's bedroom phone was bugged and the recording device was in the next bedroom. That was an amateur's job... crude, but I guess, effective."

"Any way you can find out who ordered and paid for the camera installation?"

"Naturally. But it will require the services of an independent hacker. Not cheap, my friend."

"Do it. We need to know."

George returned to the kitchen and relayed the information. "What else did you learn about the Bielmanns?" he asked.

"I have a report on the condition of Tim Michelson's wife. Here's an email I got from the librarian." She read, "'Hi Beryl, I was just informed that last week Tim's wife collapsed and a neighbor called 9-1-1 and the paramedics came and took her to the hospital. She wasn't coherent. Tim signed the papers to put her on a kidney dialysis machine; and during the procedure she became fully conscious and got violent and the attorney for the faith healing church came at her behest and the hospital stalled him but was forced to discontinue the nearly completed session. The physicians agreed that if she hadn't been treated at the time that they intervened, she would have gone into uremic poisoning or something like that - my source wasn't sure and naturally the hospital records are sacrosanct.'"

"When was this?" Sensei asked.

"She just said, 'Last week,'" Beryl answered.

"I wonder why nobody let us know," George said.

"Is his wife a member of that religion founded by Mary Baker Eddy," Sensei asked.

Beryl shook her head. "No, she belongs to another kind of faith healing group. Evidently there are thousands of different groups."

"Let's get back to Tim. I think we can write him off as a suspect," Sensei said. "What motive would he have?"

"None. His father, his children, and he, himself, now live in the main house. Tim has no other employment, but his bills all seem to be paid. His children go to private day school and he drives a nice car. Why would he want to disturb the status quo?"

"And," Beryl added, "he will probably marry the heiress. He's sleeping with her now. For all we know another Michelson generation is in the pipeline.

"The Bielmanns want to use Tim's relationship with Heidi to prove that she's incompetent. This pretended spinal injury and her need to be in a wheelchair may give Heidi the excuse to keep Tim there - that's true. But to enable him to be free to care for her, Heidi has actively supported the faith-ministry. This makes her look just as crazy as his wife. And their intimate relationship while she's in a wheelchair makes him look like a monster who takes sexual advantage of a mentally ill girl who is also physically disabled. Think about the picture of him putting a crazed, paralyzed girl in his bed. That is the image that the Bielmanns will want to show the court.

"Unless, of course, Tim and Heidi say that they want to wait a year for proprieties' sake. But if she's pregnant, we can all forget propriety."

Sensei laughed. "Families. I hate to climb out of this gene pool, but I have to go back to the temple to write this week's Dharma talk."

Sensei Percy Wong, aside from being a Zen Buddhist priest, was a well known karate master. He held formal classes in the Recreation Center of a large Methodist Church in another county, but he kept in shape and taught a few private students - Beryl among them - in his private dojo - a room that was built above his garage.

After the meeting with George and Sensei, Beryl did some marketing and housework, changed her clothes, and went to the temple to take a private karate lesson. She finished at five o'clock and returned to her apartment, to eat, bathe, and dress for evening services at the temple. George, claiming to have a headache, did not attend services.

By eight-thirty the service was over. As Sensei locked the temple doors, Beryl made tea in the small ground floor kitchen. After tea and a muffin, she returned to her office/residence half a block away.

The office phone was ringing as she opened the front office door.

V. Bruce Galeen was calling from the hospital in Media. "I called before but didn't leave a message. I don't know if you know that there's been a serious incident at Black Walnut Farm. Hiram Bielmann was shot and Heidi got pushed down the stairs in her wheelchair."

Beryl gasped. "No! We know nothing about it. What happened?"

"Tim Michelson found Hiram lying on the foyer staircase - he had been shot in the head; and he found Heidi unconscious at the foot of the stairs. Evidently she was sitting in her wheelchair when it was pushed down the stairs. Hiram is in intensive care and she's in the spinal surgery wing in Memorial hospital. He's in a coma and she's in and out of consciousness."

"What time was all this? What details do you have?"

"I wrote the chronology down as I got it from Tim. Everybody except Heidi went into town early. It's Election Day. The servants had the day off. Tim drove them to town. There were four of them who reside at the Farm. Hiram and Loreen drove in separate cars. Tim and his father met with the architect who said he wanted to look at the site before he began a discussion about buildings. He made an appointment to come next week and meet with the parties. So as soon as Hiram got there he called Loreen in her car and they both came home. Tim's wife was feeling better after she had a dialysis treatment and wanted to keep the kids to watch a movie. Tim took his father to vote and they went home to Black Walnut. His father was tired and achy and needed to rest. Tim talked to Heidi and then went to pick up his kids."

"When was this?" Beryl asked.

"Three o'clock. He got his kids, made a short trip to show them the carnival, and came home. As he parked, the kids ran in the house and started to scream. Tim hurried in and found Heidi on the floor and Hiram bleeding up on the steps. That was around 4:45 or 4:50. He checked them and called 9-1-1. That was at 4:55. Then he ran out to look for Loreen. He didn't know if she was dead or injured someplace. His father was sound asleep in bed.

"He found Loreen back near the stables. She knew nothing. The paramedics took Heidi and her father to the hospital. Heidi's in the Spinal Injury section and Hiram's - I don't know! - they're both being moved around. He's a gun shot victim. He was shot in the right temple or forehead. I can't be certain about this but I don't think the bullet exited his head - so maybe he was shot in the eye. What do I know? I'm an estate attorney."

"Is he still being worked on by the doctors?"

"They just brought him down. His head looks like it's in a cocoon. But he's still breathing. I think most of the work they did was imaging work - that's what I overheard one nurse say. And the police went back to Black Walnut Farm to secure the scene or some damned thing.

"Tim took his kids back to his wife's house and then he and Loreen Bielmann went to police headquarters. They didn't bring old Michelson in. They could barely wake him up. He had taken his pain medication and didn't hear or see anything. After Tim and Loreen gave their statements, they went to Memorial Hospital - where Heidi and Hiram had been taken. Loreen Bielmann called me. I told her I'm not a criminal attorney but I came down as a courtesy. I stayed with her until Hiram was brought down. She was terrified that he'd die in surgery or something.

"And then I remembered that my secretary told her to contact Wagner & Tilson... as if I knew George Wagner personally. I thought I ought to call you to keep you informed. I'm leaving now to return home. This place is a madhouse. Take down my private phone and call me if you hear anything." He recited his private number.

"Just one thing," Beryl asked. "How is it that Loreen didn't hear anything or know what was going on... the gunshot?"

"She said that they wanted to give some of their design ideas to the architect who's supposed to draft plans for the new carriage house and stables. She needed the dimension of rooms and spaces."

"Why wasn't Hiram with her?"

"She wanted to measure something and about 4:30 he went back to the house to get a longer measuring tape or something... a long kind that winds up."

"I know what you mean... fifty feet. So the attack occurred between 4:30 and 4:50."

"Yes. That's what I figure."

"Ok, Mr. Galeen. Thank you for letting me know. I'll keep you in the loop. By the way, do you know whether Loreen hired another attorney to represent her?"

"Nobody. She says she doesn't need an attorney. She only called me because my number was in her 'call list' and the crime occurred on the estate."

Beryl called George on his land line and his cell phone. He had turned both of his phones off, and her calls went straight to voice-mail. That was unusual; but considering his earlier encounter with Lilyanne, for all she knew he was with "his Minx" and didn't want to be disturbed. Beryl left urgent messages to call her back, and then she called Sensei Percy Wong.

Sensei hurried down to the office. "Who the hell is our client?" he sensibly asked.

"Nobody. We don't have a client. It was a friendship thing. George didn't want to be compromised by an agency agreement and the Bielmanns weren't inclined to pay for an investigation. They originally wanted him to help them prove Heidi was nuts. Lily wanted him to help Heidi get them evicted and prove that they were trying to harm her."

"Where does that leave us?"

"Damned if I know. But we just can't ignore it. George isn't answering his phone. For all we know, he's with Lily. Let's at least go to the hospital and see how Heidi's doing."

The surgical resident was not happy to be approached by Beryl and Sensei. The moment he saw Beryl extend her card to him, he put up his hands. "Are you a reporter, a lawyer, or a faith-healer? Either way, I have nothing to say." He tried to walk away.

"I'm a private investigator. I have no axe to grind." Beryl smiled at him. "I work for your patient. What's going on?"

"You have no idea how much time those people take up and how much paperwork they generate. Newspaper reporters... questions."

"What's Heidi's specific injury?"

"I'm not allowed to discuss this with you," he said, amazed that she would even ask. Then he seemed to reconsider. "Are you Lily?"

"No. Why do you ask?"

"She regained consciousness for a few minutes and asked for Lily. She said she would only talk to Lily."

"Then let me try to get Lily on the phone!" Beryl took out her phone and called Tarleton House. Sanford answered. "This is Beryl," she said. "Is Lily home? But, Listen! Sanford! If she's there don't call her yet. Her friend Heidi's in serious condition at Memorial. She will speak only to Lily. But do not let Lily drive here alone. She's a new driver and–" Sanford said that he understood. Beryl ended the conversation by saying, "Fourth Floor, Spinal section."

The doctor was relieved. "If she's conscious and talking, she can make her own decisions. So far it's more of that faith healing crap from her step-mother. She refused to sign for the surgery as her nearest living relative because she says Heidi's a devout believer in faith-healing which we learned when we inquired about her spinal injury from her riding accident a few months ago."

"Trust me on this, Doctor. Heidi Bielmann does not believe in faith healing. It's one of those family ploys. But that's between you and me. Lily will get her to sign for whatever medical procedure you recommend. What's her problem?"

"I hope this doesn't put my ass on the line. As a worst case scenario, she's got what we call an Axial burst fracture with some fragmented bone and some angulation at the injury site."

"And you think that surgery would fix it?"

"Well I sure as hell don't think it would make it worse!"

"Is she in any danger of permanent paralysis?"

"Not in my opinion - not with proper care. But the sooner she gets into surgery, the better."

"All right. As long as Heidi was conscious when she requested Lily, put Lily's name down as an approved visitor - before her step-mother forbids any outside contacts. Lily will be here in a few minutes. Whatever you think needs to be done, will be done. Will you be doing the surgery?"

"No. Ainsley Fallon will do it. He's the department head."

"What other hospitals is he associated with in the area?"

"Saint Luke's. Why?"

"Heidi may be afraid to stay here. Her dad was shot and she didn't just happen to roll down the stairs in her wheelchair. We're talking attempted murder."

"Oh, shit. I forgot about that."

"Do not tell anyone - by anyone I mean anyone - that we had this conversation about possibly transferring her to Saint Luke's. It might be necessary to remove her as if she had refused traditional medical treatment and opted out for faith healing. She's determined to appear to be in accord with this 'cure by prayer' routine. It's complicated."

"It must be." He listened to his name being summoned on the public address speaker. "Call me when Lily gets here."

"Grazadei." Beryl read his name tag and smiled. "That's a strange name for someone who doesn't believe in the power of prayer." He laughed as he walked away.

"Put Lily's name on the list!" Beryl called. The doctor raised his hand and shook it, indicating that he got the message.

Sanford waited with Sensei and Beryl while Lily went into Heidi Bielmann's room. Dr. Grazadei joined them. Fifteen minutes later Lily emerged. "She's willing to have any surgery Dr. Fallon wants to perform, but not here. And she wants it to be officially recorded that she's declining to have surgery at all and that she's going to opt out for faith healing."

Beryl stood up. "Since she's lucid, let her sign herself out. She probably has insurance to pay for these hospital charges. Then you can order her admission to Saint Luke's under the name of Beryl Tilson... that's my name. All her bills will be paid in cash immediately. Right?" Beryl looked at Lily.

"No problem. I'll have my father pay, and Heidi's accountants will reimburse him. Heidi Bielmann," she explained to Dr. Grazadei, "is an heiress. She's even richer than I am. And I'm one of the "candy-making Smiths." It was an inside joke that only Beryl and Sensei got.

Grazadei wanted to understand the joke. "What's a candy-making Smith?" he asked.

"In the religion of the aristocratic rich," said Lily, "those who get rich making candy are children of a lesser god." Grazadei smiled at her for longer than it seemed appropriate.

Beryl shook her head. "This release and admission is probably too much to dump on Dr. Grazadei. Lily, how about calling your father. Ask him to arrange the discharge of Ms. Bielmann from Memorial because she wants to see a faith healer; and the admission of Ms. Tilson to Saint Luke's for an axial burst compression fracture of the spine. If I know your father he'll know Dr. Fallon personally."

"Oh, he does. He plays golf with Ainsley Fallon." Lily got out her phone and called her father as Dr. Grazadei left to prepare release documents.

Beryl called to him, "Say that she is being released into the care of a faith healer named Swami Swahananda. This gentleman here is his assistant, Swami Shiyaofeng....ananda."

"Shi Yao Feng Ananda," Sensei mused. "I like it."

While Grazadei was in Heidi's room obtaining her signature on the documents, Dr. Fallon called. Everett Smith was arranging everything as planned. A private ambulance had been dispatched to remove the patient from the hospital.

Beryl and Sensei went to the second floor Intensive Care Unit to inquire about the prognosis of Hiram Bielmann.

Galeen had returned home and the reporters who had questioned Loreen had called in their stories and had gone. Beryl found Loreen sitting on a bench in the waiting room, alone in her vigil.

Beryl introduced herself and Sensei, too, and asked what the latest news was about Mr. Bielmann's condition. "They tell me nothing. 'As well as can be expected.' What does that mean? Who told you about the accident?"

"Bruce Galeen called me. He couldn't reach my partner George Wagner, so he called me. What a shock! We're all stunned by this. He said the bullet didn't exit his skull. Is that a good thing or a bad thing? Don't they tell you anything?"

"No. If he lives he will never see out of his right eye again!"

"Are they giving him a chance, then... even after such a terrible wound?"

"They told me about a man named Phineas Gage. It was supposed to be a famous case."

"Yes. He was a railroad worker and an explosion went off prematurely and drove a pike of some kind through his eye and out the top of his head. He lived to tell the tale. He'd go around on the talk circuit and show people his scars. Evidently he became quite the attraction."

"The doctor said that he lived a dozen years after that. Nobody knows how he managed to survive, but every person with a head injury thinks about him and wants to repeat the miracle. 'Still,' he said, 'hope never hurt a recovery.' So I guess I'm supposed to remember this railroad worker and hope that my husband survives." She began to weep so uncontrollably that Beryl had to go to the nurse's station to ask the nurse for an additional supply of tissues.

Sensei went out to speak to Beryl before she returned with the tissues. "Loreen hasn't asked about Heidi and it's probably just as well that we don't lie to her. Let's just leave the tissues and tell her that we are on another case, and this was George's case so in his absence we paid a courtesy call."

"Good idea. I don't want to get her mind involved with Heidi's prognosis." She looked at her watch. "It's midnight. Let's find out how Heidi's doing at Saint Luke's and go home."

WEDNESDAY, NOVEMBER 9, 2011

George arrived at the office before Beryl awakened. He went upstairs to her apartment, knocked loudly until he heard her answer, then let himself in. He was angry. "What the hell is going on?"

Beryl looked at the clock on her bedside table. "Seven? What are you on? The graveyard shift? You turned your phone off early. Don't come in here demanding to know what's going on. I left you messages."

"The phones here are off too! Bruce Galeen had someone come to my house to knock on the door and tell me to call him! He just learned that Heidi checked herself out of the hospital. I didn't even know she was in the hospital. Attempted murder? Hiram was shot in the head and Heidi pushed down a staircase and I didn't know shit. You could have come to my house last night when he called you. You could have woke me up!"

"Bullshit!" Beryl snarled. "Sensei was with me. It was eight thirty. Both your phones were off. We had to act fast. We weren't gonna drive up to your house just to find you zonked out with your pain medication or coveting your privacy with Lilyanne. What did we know? I called and left messages. If you don't pick up your messages that's not my fault."

"What the hell do you mean? My 'privacy with Lilyanne'?"

"Jesus, George, she was all over you yesterday afternoon. What were Sensei and I supposed to think was the reason you were offline at 8:30?"

"So all this goes on and I'm kept in the dark?"

"Go down and make tea. And don't go banging on Sensei's door. He and I didn't get back until 2 a.m. *We were working until 2 a.m. which is why our phones are off.*"

Beryl took her time showering and dressing. She was too tired to rush and too annoyed with George to hurry on his account.

Finally, she came downstairs and went into the office kitchen. George pursed his lips and looked at her sideways. "I shut the phone off to be with Lily? Is that what you thought? Where is your brain?"

"It was a possibility. We didn't know what to think. 8:30? Your phone is off at 8:30?"

"So tell me what happened. Start from the beginning and don't leave anything out!"

Beryl sighed and made a serious effort to compose herself. In a soft, deliberate voice she related the events as Bruce Galeen had given them to her, and then she added an account of the events at the hospital. "Heidi needed immediate surgery, but Loreen had refused to sign for it because she said Heidi believed in faith healing. The surgical resident said that the sooner they do this kind of surgery the better it is. I did what I could to facilitate that.

"At the hospital, Heidi briefly regained consciousness and asked for Lily, saying that she would talk only to Lily. I called Lily. When Sanford answered I told him not to let her drive alone since she was too inexperienced to drive in an emotional emergency. He agreed and brought her. She went in to talk to Heidi and it was agreed that her surgeon, Ainsley Fallon, would in fact operate on her but in another hospital and under my name. Lily's father arranged everything.

"Heidi was released from Memorial because she refused further treatment. She was released in the care of Swami Swahananda via his assistant, Swami Shi Yao Feng Ananda, a.k.a. Sensei Percy Wong. Lily's father ordered a private ambulance to take her to Saint Luke's; and since Mr. Smith personally knew Ainsley Fallon, everything was set up by the two of them. That is it."

"Swami Swahananda? So people think she's under my care? What's the point of that?"

"She's scared. Her father was shot. Somebody pushed her down the stairs. One of her vertebra is fractured. What the hell do you want?"

"All right!. All right! What ultimately is the plan?"

"Since she doesn't want anyone to know that she's having surgery—"

"Wait a minute! Why is she still persisting in this phony faith healing routine?"

"Sometimes you can be so dense! How can she say she suddenly believes in modern medicine? She was a girl who could walk fine but said she had a spinal injury that she was trying to cure with religious interventions so that she could have the boyfriend stay with her. Now she's got a real spinal injury. She has to keep up the pretense since to admit the truth would make a liar out of Tim, too. She regards him as her protector. That's what she pays him for... sex and protection." Exasperated, Beryl threw up her hands. "If she started seeing doctors and walking around, what work could she pay Tim to do? Be her paid companion? Have you been reading Jane Austen again?"

"Someday... someday..." George looked heavenward.

"Also, as long as she says she believes in faith healing she can have you around. *Why* she thinks that would be of benefit to her, I cannot say."

"I know only that she fears she will be vulnerable in Memorial hospital... I don't know... maybe it was her father getting shot standing next to her... or that she got pushed down a very long flight of stairs while she was sitting in a wheelchair... some silly little thing that gave her the idea that someone was being *awfully mean!*"

George's face grew red and he clenched his jaw.

Beryl continued, "She needs spinal surgery and her father got shot in his head." She wagged her finger. "Somebody needs a 'time-out'!"

George took a deep breath. "Go on."

"Since Heidi was afraid that someone would try to hurt Heidi in the hospital, she was admitted as Beryl. Now she is absolutely safe. I mean... who would want to hurt Beryl? But, Wait! If that is Beryl in the hospital, what has happened to Heidi? Ah, she is receiving faith healing treatments in a Pocono Mountain cabin retreat, a cabin that is owned by Assistant Swami Shi Yao Feng Ananda. But how can she be in two places at once? She can't be! And so Lilyanne Smith will pretend to be Heidi just as Heidi is pretending to be Beryl. Only Lily will wear a dark wig and glasses."

George's attitude changed. Beryl could not read it. "How long were you planning on carrying out this impersonation?" he asked.

"A week or two? I'm not sure how long the recovery period will take."

"Let me understand this. Heidi's in the hospital recovering from spinal surgery for a couple of weeks and I'm alone with Lily in a cabin in the woods, pretending to give her faith healing treatments, for those same weeks? Have you lost your mind?"

"Well... actually, we assumed that since there would be so much climbing mountain trails and stuff like that, Sensei would be the best man for the job. He volunteered. But, knowing you, he said that if you preferred to give the treatments, he'd bow out. But really, the best solution would be for him to play you and for you to play being a Zen monk - give us a few Dharma talks, answer your phone at 8 p.m."

George did not attempt to conceal his anger. "What the hell is wrong with you? If she's pretending to be Heidi and Heidi is on somebody's hit list, that puts Lily in danger! She's a wide-open target out there. Where is your brain? Didn't either of you think about the jeopardy you put Lily in?"

"Yes... yes, we did. We didn't like the plan at all. But Lily insisted. And she's a woman who gets her way! Stop worrying. She knows what she's doing! She's very intelligent. She may act like a ditz when she's around you, but that's just the effect you have on women. We're overwhelmed by all those muscles and brain waves." She tried to soften her response. "Don't worry. Sensei will protect her."

"From what? A ninja attack? Don't be stupid! I've been to that cabin. It's exposed. There are a dozen places where anybody with a goddamned rifle can get off a perfect shot." George groaned. He looked at his hands and asked them, "And from fifty yards away Percy's gonna do a karate chop and deflect a few incoming rifle rounds?" He groaned again. "All because I shut off my fucking phone!"

"What could you have done differently? Nothing. *Lily insisted!*"

George went into the office and called a body armor specialist. He ordered a bathrobe that was fully lined with Kevlar. He ordered a blanket that was fully lined with Kevlar. He ordered a cap to be worn under a wig - a cap made of Kevlar. And he wanted them by the next day.

Beryl called Saint Luke's hospital and asked for Beryl Tilson's room. She was connected to the nursing station in the surgery wing. "The operation was successful and Miss Tilson is doing as well as can be expected," the nurse said.

"When are visiting hours?" Beryl asked.

"I'd wait at least until the 2 p.m. visiting-hour schedule. Miss Tilson will be bright eyed and bushy tailed by then."

Beryl sat on the edge of George's desk. "So," she said softly, "who shot Hiram Bielmann and pushed Heidi down the stairs?"

George decided to be calm. "We have three known possibilities. Loreen, Tim, Tim's father. And who knows how many possible perpetrators that we haven't heard about yet."

Sensei came to the office dressed in a business suit.

"You look like a man 'on the go,'" said Beryl.

"I am that, indeed," Sensei said, straightening his tie. "I'm dressed to go to Tarleton House for lunch and a meeting. I've got an appointment with Everett Smith at 11 a.m. Any messages?"

George groaned. *"And the hits just keep on comin'."*

"We were discussing suspects," Beryl noted. "We can think of only three: Loreen, Tim, and Tim's Dad. What do you think?"

"I'm a Zen Buddhist. I only think in riddles. And then I don't try to solve them."

George glared at him. "Funny answer. You're right about the riddle," he said. "I also can't think straight. And you're going out to Tarleton to have lunch with Lily's father? Maybe you can tell him what you and Lily need for your two weeks of mountain fun. Great. Frankly, I don't give a shit. It's not my case." George got up, grabbed his jacket, and walked out of the office.

Sensei checked in with the gatekeeper at Tarleton House and drove the long curved cobblestone way up to the house. Everett Smith, having been notified by the gatekeeper, was out on the portico steps waiting for him.

"Long time, no see!" Everett smiled. "Park and come on in."

Sensei followed Everett into his study in the house. Sanford was arranging the food service in the study. Sandwiches were under a silver dome and a selection of teas waited in canisters to be placed in individual pots. Hot water simmered in a samovar.

"I've invited Sanford to join us," Everett said. "None of us is happy about Lily's decision to impersonate Heidi. My daughter, however, has a mind of her own. God knows, we've made enough bad decisions for her. How can we object?"

"I don't know her well," Sensei replied, "but from what I do know, I'd say our best course is not to oppose her decisions but to use our time to devise ways to protect her regardless of what she decides to do. Personally, I think we should hire an actress, a professional."

"I already thought of that and brought it up. Lily said absolutely not. We'd never get the right one on such short notice. And to be ethical we'd have to explain the dangers. She vetoed the idea. Tell me," Smith asked, "how does George Wagner feel about all this?"

"He's furious with Beryl and me for allowing it. He's already ordered a Kevlar blanket, a robe, and a skull cap to wear under her wig."

"Good man. Send me the bill. Do I pick the items up?"

"I don't know. I wasn't there when he ordered them. Beryl will know. I tried to call him on my way here, but he's not answering his phone. I've never seen him so angry."

"My daughter has a special fondness for him."

"Yes, Sir. I know."

"And he seems to be inordinately fond of her."

"Yes, Sir. I know."

"They have a definite chemistry. They always had."

"Yes, Sir. I know."

"You're an easy fellow to get along with."

Sanford broke into the conversation. "May I express an opinion here..."

Everett Smith chuckled as he displayed on his TV a Google map of Sensei's cabin in the Poconos. "As you can see," Sensei got up and pointed at the screen, "the cabin faces east, and access to it - up this trail, here, begins at a little parking area and goes up to the cabin porch deck and front door."

He moved his hand to an area off screen. "The asphalt road ends here at the town of Jim Thorpe, and the gravel road ends here," he pushed his finger onto the screen, "and the dirt road ends at that parking area which half a dozen cabin owners use. We can turn around and go back, but this is the end of the line for vehicles. From there, it's less than a three hundred feet climb up to my cabin. I can carry Lily that distance. I don't want her to try to walk it. It's rocky and it's slippery.

"I want her wearing as much protective clothing - not just Kevlar for protection - but long johns and wool garments for warmth. It gets very cold in the cabin. I also would like to purchase one of those sex dolls or mannikins, something full size. I can let Lily make an appearance outside the cabin in a long chair that I keep on the deck which measures, say, 9 by 12 feet in front of the cabin. I can put her in the *chaise longue* and let her show her face, and then as if we've forgotten something, I'll carry her back in. I'll come out carrying the doll. I'll put the blanket over it."

"Where on earth will we get a sex doll?" Everett Smith asked.

Sanford said, "They are sold at our local adult book store."

Smith looked surprised. "Sanford! How would you know that?"

"I've been elected by Madam's book club to pick up and take back rented pornography movies they watch during their book club hen parties."

"Nobody ever told me that! What kind of porn?"

"The usual... Homo. Straight. BDSM."

"I don't know what to say!"

"Say nothing, Sir," Sanford advised. "It gets a man nowhere to try to interfere with hen parties."

"My wife rents porn movies?"

"No sir, your butler does."

Sensei cleared his throat. "The cabin?"

"We'll have Sanford pick you up one of those sex dolls, and a dark wig, and put one of those big turtle-neck sweaters on it to hide most of the face. And I think that Sanford and I will be staying at a Lodge near Jim Thorpe, Pennsylvania. We'll dress in those Indian garments. What do you think?"

"Will you be visiting the cabin every day?"

"Yes. We plan to bring you your meals. We'll drive back here every morning and pick up your lunch and dinner, and then drive back up. Do you have a microwave oven in your cabin?"

"I don't even have electricity in my cabin."

"Do you have a stove in your cabin?"

"Yes. There's an aperture in the top of the stove for putting a frying pan or pot or even an oven-box. Just be sure it isn't served in plastic."

"Excellent. I'll tell the cook to use those Pyrex covered dishes. I want my girl to eat well while she's up there."

Sensei poured tea. "I'd suggest that you not dress in Indian garments, but try to look more like Christian ministers. You could say that you're observing faith healing techniques to use with your own flocks or something like that. Neither of you looks particularly Indian; and you'll only create hostile interest if you look like a couple of fake foreigners. Given yoga's popularity, someone may ask for advice about doing a *Suryanamaskar*. You also probably don't speak Hindi and you'd be in a spot if someone at the lodge addressed you in your native language."

"Christian, it is. I wanted to hire some bodyguards with rifles who could watch the cabin from a distance. What do you think?"

"They won't know the parties. The risk of 'friendly fire' or of falling into a dependent state of mind, of letting *them* be on guard instead of us, is too great. I don't think it's necessary or desirable. The food, yes. I can bring my laptop and Lily can bring hers. We can watch one while you take the other to be recharged. You can select some DVD's - no porn, please... but the kind of movies Lily likes. And be sure you refer to her as Heidi Bielmann when you speak about her at the lodge. Word will get out that Heidi is being treated by faith healers and that will cause reporters to snoop which is good. Whenever you speak, always suppose that someone else is listening."

They ate their sandwiches and then, while Sensei talked to the cook about menus, Smith and his butler left to go to the Christian supply store to buy shirts with turn-around collars.

Beryl visited Heidi in her room. "It was strange," she said, "asking to visit myself. How do you feel?"

"I'm fine, surprisingly so. Dr. Fallon operated on me last night. Right after you left, I was CAT scanned and prepped and taken to the O.R. for major surgery. Lily and I hoped that that adorable Dr. Grazadei would assist, but it was a lady resident who helped."

"How long were you in surgery."

"I think it took a few hours... maybe four. I'm not sure. You know what they used? It isn't crazy glue. It's something else. There's a brochure on the table over there. Can you reach it?"

Beryl opened the brochure and read about *Vertebroplasty*: "Wow. So they inject an acrylic bone cement called 'polymethylmethacrylate' - that's some name - an acrylic bone cement. They put it right on or in the damaged bone. You'll be out of here sooner than we thought."

"Yes, I'll be fitted for a corset - a back brace thing, tomorrow. Velcro closures. They are made to order so it will take ten days or so to get it. If all goes well, in a few days I'll be taped up and made to walk to the bathroom. I'll be glad to get the catheter out of me."

"I know the feeling."

"Have you heard how my dad is doing?"

"Only that he's in intensive care and his condition is very serious."

"Does Tim know I'm here?"

"No. Nobody knows - not Tim or the police. Just your doctors and Lily and I and my partners. The hospital staff thinks you're Beryl Tilson. A cashier's check was delivered to the hospital's accounting department this morning. You're in good financial standing. So, tell me... now that you are, as the nurse put it, 'bright eyed and bushy tailed,' what happened at the house yesterday."

"I've gone over this a thousand times. The police tried to question me at Memorial Hospital. All I know is that I was upstairs and my dad came up to see how I was feeling. I had told him the reason I couldn't go into town to vote was that my stomach was upset. He had teased me about having morning sickness. I told him I was feeling better and wanted to go down to the kitchen and get something to eat. The cook wasn't on duty. He helped me get into my chair. What we do is push me to the stairs and then back up the chair and park it against the wall so that it's out of the way of people walking. Then Angus comes up and gets me. Angus wasn't there so my dad was going to carry me down. He wheeled me to the top of the stairs and then started to rotate the chair to back it up to the wall. But the old wicker chair isn't so maneuverable. If you want to turn it, you sort of have to pivot it on one wheel and grab the other wheel and pull. He bent over to grab the wheel and then he shouted, 'What are you doing with that?' A gun fired as I was pushed and went tumbling down the stairs. The police told me that my dad was hit in his right front forehead. The bullet went in but it didn't come out."

Beryl asked, "What side of you was your father on?"

"Behind me on my left. I felt the push coming from the right side back of the chair."

"If the gunshot came first, it suggests that there were two people or one who is left handed. Is anyone left handed?"

"Nobody who lives at Black Walnut Farm is left handed."

"Let me set this up. You are sitting. Your father is standing behind you on your left. Could there be a person on your father's left... beside him?"

"No. The person who shot had to be behind us and I suppose came out of the right side of the hall since my room is on the left side as is Mr. Michelson's, and all the doors on that side were shut."

"If a right handed person comes from the right side and simultaneously pushes a wheelchair and fires a gun, he would have to cross his arms. Push you with his left hand and shoot the gun with his right. It doesn't make sense."

"That's what the police say. There had to be two people. I didn't see anyone, but for all I know there were three or four. The carpeting is deep up there."

"Jeff Gable said that the monitor for the wall lamp cameras is locked in a china cabinet in the dining room which is directly under your bedroom. As soon as the police take down the yellow tape, I'll go out to Black Walnut and get Tim's father to let me in. I'll pick the cabinet's lock and see if the incident was captured by the cameras. If the would-be killer knows about those cameras, he or she will remove the recording fast. If the monitor is gone, I'd like to engage a hacker to break into the installer's system and see if we can retrieve footage from the shooting incident. I've already asked a hacker to determine who ordered the surveillance. But that was just routine bookkeeping system hacking. This will involve creating a duplicate of video records - if they exist. It will be expensive."

"By all means, do it. I'd like to see what happened, too, so don't destroy the recording until I've seen it."

"The police didn't recover the gun. Do you know if there was a gun in the house?"

"Yes. My grandfather gave my mother a .38 caliber revolver. It wasn't a secret. When she left my father put it in the attic to keep it out of reach of Loreen's kids."

"Did people come and go in the house? Were the Bielmanns the party-giving type?"

"No. The Bielmann family lost their money - but that was after my mom and dad were married." Heidi smiled. "Unless you've got an honorable excuse - like being a member of the clergy or the military, you're excommunicated 'without prejudice' as the CIA says. This means you don't get booted off the Register but you are no longer invited to parties because you can't reciprocate. And naturally you can't afford to participate in social events, like a debutante's 'coming out' party, or private schools, and so on. My father remained a member of his gentlemen's club. He continued to pay his dues and fees. But he and Loreen were not on anybody's invitation list. Dad's friends were loyal to my mother and he was known as a philanderer. And also, Loreen was not a member of society."

"Let's talk more about your relationship with your dad and Loreen. What drove you to try to evict them?"

"They did. It's my house. My father got plenty out of the divorce. My mom's parents owned the estate but they had given it to my mom and dad for a wedding present. He tells people he gave her his half of the property. He didn't give her anything. She gave him millions for his half. Because he continued to live in the house, I gave him access to the estate accounts. When I was in the convent they just raided the accounts for fantastic sums. And when I came back, they refused to recognize me as the owner of the house. I was the unwanted guest that needed to be forced out."

"You say, 'they.' Do you mean that both Loreen and your father could sign checks, or just your father?"

"Just my father. But he approved everything she did."

"Ok. Give me some examples of how they refused to recognize your position."

"Except for Tim's father, the servants were all new. They must have been told I was a lunatic who could safely be ignored. Loreen had hired a cook and gave her weekly menu instructions. I said, 'I don't like this... or I don't want that served.' The cook would say, 'Madam has requested it.' I'd say, 'I am paying your salary, not Madam.' Sausages, for example, I think are disgusting. I would say, 'Do not purchase or serve sausages!' But again and again she would serve sausages. We used to buy eggs from a farmer down the road, a man who had been a family friend for years. She started buying eggs from a store in town. I said, 'I want the eggs from Fairmont Farm.' The cook said, 'Madam prefers other eggs.' I called Fairmont Farm and told them to deliver two dozen eggs. The cook refused to accept them.

"The kids would do things to harass me. I'd go out to ride and all the bridles would be gone... hidden by them. They'd sneak into my bedroom and take things. They'd steal one shoe from a pair of my shoes. They broke my glasses... stepped on them 'by accident.' I was in the bathtub once and the youngest one, Gordon, had just gotten a new video camera. He hid in my closet and began to film me while I was naked. I was furious. I chased that kid down the hall and tackled him and used an old iron doorstop to smash that camera to bits. Two days later I had my riding accident - which was no accident. I had a thin line bruise across my chest. A couple of inches higher, and it would have broken my neck.

"They lavished money on those rotten kids. Each kid has his or her own computer, phone, and TV DSL line, and a box-thing that plays video games, and a scanner, and a printer. And they didn't take care of anything. The oldest kid got a new Corvette for his sixteenth birthday. They hated that Mr. Michelson lived upstairs. And they threatened to publish on the internet photos they had secretly taken of Tim and me in bed. I have no doubt that they would carry out the threat.

"Anyway, one day at lunch, sausages were served. I snapped. I got up from the table and called my accountant on the hall phone. I instructed him to cancel all credit cards and accounts as of that moment. Checks that were returned to the payees would be re-issued by me - they just had to contact me and present a valid invoice. The bank was to cancel any automatic payouts they made until I personally made new arrangements for automatic payouts. And then I went out to my car, drove to the bank, closed all the estate accounts and opened new ones, including a new personal account of mine. All in my name alone. Loreen and my father had made investments in their name, using my estate money. Tim's father heard them talking about covering one of their losses with estate money, so I called Bruce Galeen - I've known him for years - and he handled putting a stop on that investment account. They had gotten snookered in a Ponzi scheme. But they still had other investments they had made before that cut-off date. I followed all this up with certified mail. I gave the cook a month's severance pay and told her to leave immediately. And I told the others, including my father, to find another place to live. I told him I would file eviction papers."

"Who was the stock broker?" Beryl asked.

"Thompson & Associates. Mr. Thompson was very apologetic. But what was done, was finished. My father had gone through hundreds of thousands of dollars. I know that sounds incredible, but it's true. In the few years I was away he and Loreen squandered a fortune. My mother had been more than generous to him mostly because she knew she was ill - she had lung trouble which proved to be cancer. She wanted me to stay here. She went back to where she grew up. Besides, the "mile-high" city is supposed to be good for lung problems. *Magic Mountain*, Thomas Mann stuff. When the altitude didn't help her, she transferred ownership of nearly everything to me. She was too sick to manage the finances."

"What made you leave the convent?"

"After my brother killed himself, I entered the convent and Tim got married. Tim's dad was my only contact with the outside world. We exchanged letters. He told me about Tim's wife and how miserable Tim was. I had always had a crush on Tim. I just couldn't stop thinking about him. So I came home. It was Mr. Michelson who drove down to West Virginia and picked me up.

"There's always gossip that involves one of us. I saw in one of the gossip columns that people are speculating about an affair between Tim and Loreen."

"Good grief!"

Heidi laughed. "Yes, Tim and Loreen are suspected of being more than just 'friends.' I wonder how Tim's taking that! He drove Loreen into town a few times when she had an infected toe from getting a pedicure. I guess people saw them in the same car and that made them lovers. And also his wife has experienced a miracle. She had a dialysis treatment and was seen in the market looking 'hale and hearty.' A reporter asked one of the police detectives if she was considered a suspect. The answer was, 'no comment.'" Heidi yawned. "No comment. How stupid."

Beryl patted her hand. "I think you need to sleep right now. I'll go out to the 'crime scene' and see if they've removed the tape, and if so I'll try to look at the monitor and pull a copy of what's been recorded. I'll make sure that Loreen and Tim are out of the house. If someone tells you that there's a woman roaming around your property, you'll know it's only me. Ok. Get some rest and I'll take to you later."

"Will Swami Swahananda come and visit me?"

"I will definitely ask him to do that."

George gassed up the pickup and got onto the Pennsylvania Turnpike. He neither knew nor cared where he was going. He just wanted to escape. He sought distance, not direction.

He passed the place that Beryl said was the exit that led to Lily's convent. He crossed the state line and entered Ohio. It was time to stop for the night. His vision was beginning to blur.

He exited the highway and checked into a motel. He went to his room and realized that he forgot to bring his medications. His knee ached from holding it in a static sitting position. His arm and fingers ached from holding the wheel. He took a hot shower, toweled off, and got into bed, determined to do a deep relaxation exercise to relieve the pain. He did a few cycles of a deep breathing technique, but he could not keep his mind focussed. He did not want to think about Lily. He had no future with Lily. He should never have allowed himself to become fascinated by a girl who was twenty years younger than he and a million times richer. Her image clamored for his attention and he could not relax.

At such times, he was supposed to employ fierce determination and substitute another topic. He was supposed to choose a pleasant topic. Instead his mind returned to the night he received the wounds that changed his life.

On that night, ten years before, George Wagner was an investigator with the Philadelphia Police. He and his partner had been ambushed on the docks in South Philadelphia. His partner was killed instantly and George had been shot in the left knee and right brachial plexus. Both injuries were excruciatingly painful and required a total of twenty-two surgeries over the next year. After his seventh surgery his wife stopped coming to visit him. He couldn't blame her. He always was drugged and rarely was even consciously aware of her presence. By his fourteenth procedure she had filed for divorce. By his eighteenth surgery she had married a man whose wealth made child support payments unnecessary, or so her attorney told him when he agreed to give her full custody. He did refuse to allow her new husband to adopt his children. She took the two kids to Northern California and left him their house and her orchid collection. After his twenty-second surgery he was so addicted to opiates that he was sent to a special drug rehab facility in Southern California. During the year that he was in rehab, she never once visited him. He'd call and she wouldn't allow the children to speak to him. Within a couple of years, the kids were old enough to answer the phone and Beryl got him a video laptop. His ex-wife did not want to put the kids on the screen but George involved California authorities and she was forced to relent. He went west several times a year to spend weekends with the kids. But now the kids were teenagers and had lives of their own. George was painfully alone.

The muscles of his right arm had gotten flaccid. They withered slightly from disuse. His knee could not be kept for a long period in a bent position. Going to the movies was an impossibility unless he sat on the aisle and could stretch out his leg. His right arm would never be the same.

Alone in the motel room, he could feel bitterness and pain latch onto him and he wanted to shake them off. He tried to rid himself of the memories by turning on the television and staring at the moving images - ordinarily a good meditation technique. He turned off the sound and watched the silent pictures roll by. His mind continued to jump from thought to thought until, finally, the room began to darken and the figures on the screen performed for eyes that had closed.

THURSDAY, NOVEMBER 10, 2011

George had neglected to close the drapes when he went to bed and now, in the cold grey November morning, a harsh square of light confronted him as he struggled to stay asleep.

He called the desk and asked the clerk to put through a call to his office. He had not brought his cellphone. Not being reachable but being able to reach gave him a feeling of control. He needed to think independently, without being prejudiced or nagged by other people. He decided that if he did not like what he heard during the call, he would simply hang up. Beryl answered the phone.

"Did I wake you up?" he asked.

"No. The phone did. Actually I was starting to wake up. You sort of pushed me over the line. Where are you?"

"Ohio."

"Before you get huffy and hang up on me, tell me where you ordered the Kevlar material. I didn't want to have to call around and Everett Smith wants to take it up to the cabin today."

"I called Liney's. Bill took the order. I said I needed it immediately and he agreed to accommodate me. How is the case?"

"Moving forward. Heidi had back surgery. She was admitted under my name at Saint Luke's. Hiram is still in grave condition. Nobody knows which way he'll go. I don't know why they haven't operated yet. It's a complicated business; and also, brain surgery is expensive. Maybe they've stayed true to form and are claiming to be too poor to pay for the surgery. The patient passes himself off as master of a forty room house. He can't then be regarded as indigent. But maybe there is a sound medical reason for letting the bullet make a home in his brain."

"How is Sensei?"

"On cloud nine. Madly in love. The love of his life, the one and only Sonya Lee sent him an invitation to take her to a Thanksgiving Dinner in San Diego. He wants to hurry up and solve this case. Nothing is allowed to interfere with his dinner with the exquisite Miss Lee."

"Is she still promising to kick his ass?"

"He received a formal invitation... something from the diplomatic corps. I doubt that it said, 'You are cordially invited to attend the ass kicking contest of Miss Sonya Lee and the Reverend Shi Yao Feng.' He bought a ballroom dance DVD to practice the steps in his cabin."

"He can practice with Lily."

"George, there are many roles that Lily can fill, but standing in for Sonya Lee is not one of them. He wants to learn to dance better than he already knows. Lily can't help him. Sonya is a professional operative... a highly trained martial artist. I'd love to see the two of them do one of those French Apache dances... to Ravel's *Bolero*."

George laughed. "I guess the two of them could clear out a room. So is there any other news?"

"Lily asks for you."

"Bullshit."

"When are you coming home?"

"I'm in a blue funk. I need to rack up some miles. I forgot my pills but fatigue got me through without them. Listen, can you keep my plants watered? At my house and in the office."

"Sure. When will you call me again?"

"I don't know. I've been thinking about driving out to see my kids. I want to see them in person."

"The Donner Pass may be closed."

"I'll head south. Maybe I'll cross the Mississippi at Saint Louis. Maybe not."

"You can at least call me when you check into a motel for the night.. or in the morning. I worry about you."

"Don't. Ok. That's it for now." He hung up the phone and took a shower.

Everett Smith and Sanford, both dressed in clerical garb, and Sensei wearing a Nehru jacket and pants, drove to the cabin in a van. Lily, wearing her wig and glasses, sat on the back seat beside her father until they reached the point in the road at which it was no longer possible to proceed by car. For the benefit of anyone who might be watching, Sensei and Sanford unloaded a stretcher, laid a six inch deep piece of memory foam on it as a mattress, carefully placed Lily on it, and carried her up to the cabin. Repeatedly they returned to the van to carry up all the needed supplies: food, dishes, cleaning supplies, bed linens, blankets, lamp oil, candles, insecticides, bullet proof "rag" armor; a deflated sex doll, laptops, games including chess and Scrabble, charcoal briquets, among other items.

Exhausted, Everett Smith leaned against the door jamb. "Sanford and I will be nearby at the Lodge. Call us any time for anything you need. We'll be back with your lunch and dinner tomorrow around noon," Everett said. "Get a good night's rest, both of you."

"Daddy," Lily called as Smith turned to wave good bye, "Please tell George to come."

"I will, my angel, I will."

"Somehow, Sir," Sanford said as they walked down to the van, "our religious raiment seems appropriate. I feel the need to pray."

Beryl had already called Mr. Michelson and told him she would be there later and that neither his son nor Loreen Bielmann was to be told of her visit. He understood. She waited at the same hilltop that George had waited on the day of the installation. The yellow tape had been removed. No police cars were in sight.

She watched Loreen's Mercedes leave. Fifteen minutes passed while the Escalade remained parked in front of the house. She knew from experience that a stakeout required more than patience. While waiting for something to happen, she could not watch with an active mind. The expectation would agitate thoughts, and the event's proximate and ultimate causes would carom off each other. Zen training had helped her to acquire an alert but static focus, a kind of 'no mind' that did not create anxiety or restlessness or even the wish that something would happen so that she could proceed to do something else. "Time to get myself into a stakeout meditation zone," she said aloud. She found a rock she could sit on and observe the scene without disturbing her vantage point. An hour later, she saw Tim leave the house and get into the Escalade. There were servants in the house, she thought; but they were not involved in the case. As soon as the car turned onto the road, she drove directly to the house and parked her car.

Angus answered the door. She asked for Mr. Michelson - Senior - who came down the steps. He knew why she was there but he nevertheless asked, "May I help you?"

"I'm here to pick up something for Miss Bielmann. It's in the dining room."

"Ah, yes," he said. "Come on and follow me."

Michelson led her back to the dining room. Beryl was prepared to pick the lock, but the cabinet's doors were open. There was no equipment inside it. The old man thought a minute, "You know... if I'm not mistaken Loreen could have carried something out of here under her coat. At least that's how it looked to me. Could that have been what you're looking for?"

"It probably was." Beryl thanked him and left. As she drove back to the highway she called Jeff Gable. "The monitor is gone. I'm told that it was probably taken away less than an hour ago. Any chance that your friend can try to retrieve the video record if the equipment was returned to CSI?"

"If she planned the crime, she might have shut down the system before hand. There's no guarantee that the file will contain the record you're looking for."

"We really don't have an alternative. See if he's able to do it. My client has already agreed to pay for the service," Beryl said.

"Will do... but I don't have to tell you, it's gonna be expensive. I take it that you'll want the complete data file. The guy who does these jobs factors in the cost of legal defense in case he's caught."

"Reassure him that the installation was illegal in the first place. He's working for the owner. CSI had no legal authority to install them. All your guy has to worry about is hacking into the surveillance company. He's reasonably safe with that leverage."

Beryl drove to Memorial hospital. Loreen Bielmann nervously paced the entrance sidewalk, smoking a cigarette.

"How is Mr. Bielmann doing?" Beryl asked.

"Only God knows, and he's not talking. These people tell you nothing, and if you want to smoke, you have to leave the hospital. They don't even have smoking rooms."

"There is no justice in this world. How is your husband? Better? Worse? Same?"

"The same, I guess. They are hopeful so far because no cascade has started. What in God's name is a cascade?"

"All I know," Beryl said, "and I'm not sure about this, is that a cascade is a kind of chain reaction. Things may look fine on the surface, but underneath, some minor thing may be happening that nobody knows about. And this small thing triggers another larger or two larger things, and these in turn cause something else to go wrong until you have a whole array of problems. So what they were saying is that this process hasn't started which is certainly good news."

"Why couldn't they just tell me that!" Loreen snapped. "Why do I have to stand out here on the sidewalk and be told what is going on with my husband?" She dropped her cigarette and stamped on it. "Bunch of incompetent fools."

"Sometimes they just can't see how things look from the other side... the side of the person who is faced with losing a loved one."

"I didn't mean to snap at you," Loreen said. "I am just so worried about him. Now they want to know about his insurance. My ex-husband was supposed to give me and the children full coverage. I understood that this included spousal coverage. Apparently it does not! Do you know where Heidi is? I know she signed herself out of the hospital again to get faith healing treatments. If she won't guarantee her father's medical bills they may have to move him to another hospital, one for poor people!"

Beryl could easily see that Loreen Bielmann's concern for her husband was genuine. What she could not easily see was the reason for Loreen's excessive concern. Not once had Loreen said the usual, "What will I do without him?" spousal lament. "This is a county hospital," she said. "Insurance or no insurance, your husband will be cared for here. He won't be moved. They should have explained that to you, too."

"Please... please... if you find out where Heidi is getting her treatments, let me know. One word from her is all it will take for them to continue giving my husband the best of all possible care. He's got to survive this awful thing that's happened. He's simply got to hang in there and fight."

"If I encounter Heidi or learn where she is, I'll let you know."

As Beryl returned to her car, her cellphone rang. Librarian Martha Myers wanted to know if Beryl or anyone in her office had ordered a set of photographs of Hiram Bielmann from Valmont Prep."

"No. I received the ones you sent on Saturday."

"Well, the most peculiar thing happened. I ordered a set on Saturday, November 5th and someone else had ordered the same set yesterday, November 10th. I got mine, but then the bookkeeper at Valmont - she's an old acquaintance of mine - saw this other order and thought it might have been an error in duplication or if not, it might be a matter of interest to me. I mean... really.... Thirty years or so pass and nobody's interested in Hiram Bielmann and then suddenly two people want the same set of photos?"

"Who purchased the other set?"

"Nobody knows, yet. If you don't purchase the photographs using a credit card and you don't pay in advance, you have to show up at the desk, pay for them, and wait a few minutes until they're produced.

"The bookkeeper told me that the woman who wanted the photographs said she'd be in to pick them up this afternoon or Monday morning. She'd pay cash for the set."

"I would love to see who picks them up. I'll drive out to Valmont's administration's offices immediately, and park near the entrance and wait to see if I can recognize the person who gets them. I hate to impose on you further, but I'd like to call you when I get there to be sure that they weren't just picked up - and I missed the action. Would it be too much trouble to ask you to check with your friend again when I call you?"

"Not at all. This is so mysterious - especially now after the attempted murder. I find it ever so exciting!"

Beryl checked the school's business hours. Nine to Four, Monday through Friday. She got directions and drove to the school's parking lot. She called Martha Myers who called the bookkeeper and learned that no one had as yet picked up the order.

Beryl looked toward the school's offices and saw a woman standing at the window waving to her. Assuming that it was the bookkeeper, she waved back.

When the offices closed at four o'clock, the photocopies still had not been picked up. Monday would be another stakeout day.

Heidi was watching the evening news as Beryl entered her room. "How are we doing?" Beryl asked.

"I'm so happy to speak to someone who knows who I am," Heidi said. "Would you do me a favor and call Memorial and ask how my dad is doing?"

Beryl called and learned that Hiram Bielmann's condition was still unchanged. She thanked the nurse and said to Heidi, "No news is good news."

"What's going on with the case?"

"I hope you're prepared for an expensive investigation. You were a little groggy when I told you about the hacker, so I'll tell you again. We asked an anonymous hacker to find out who ordered and paid for the cameras that were spying on you. This was illegal, but so were the surveillance cameras. We have a major problem. The monitor of the old system that was in the master bedroom is gone. Loreen removed it this morning. So, our only hope is to access the other company's work product files and hope they've retained a copy of the video recordings. I think it's worth a shot. Someone's trying to kill you. The hacking will have a big price tag. I'm talking thousands."

"What's my life worth?"

"That's my attitude towards this business. As long as you can pay for it and the cameras were illegally installed inside your home, that CSI company doesn't have clean hands. If it ever comes to light, they can bitch and moan in private all they want."

"I'll call my accountant now and ask him to issue Wagner & Tilson a check for whatever it costs. He can call it a consultation fee. Since I'm Beryl, how about letting me call him now on your phone."

Beryl gave her the phone and listened to Heidi instruct him with crisp efficiency. "You'll have the check delivered immediately to the offices of Wagner & Tilson, Private Investigators." She concluded the call.

"Now," Heidi laughed, "I know that you're doing well after my spinal surgery, but how am I doing with those faith healing treatments?"

Beryl shook her head and grinned. "Two ministers, the Reverends Smith and Sanford, visit you and Assistant-Swami Shiyaofeng-ananda every day. The ministers are studying the Swami's techniques. They are staying down at the lodge in Jim Thorpe, Pennsylvania - the place nearest Sensei's cabin, where they can be easily overheard commenting about your progress. They report that Swami has every hope that your health will be completely restored. Also, they say that Lily sends her love.

"I need to ask you if you've ever seen childhood photographs of your parents?"

"When my mother died, I went to Denver. At an aunt's house I saw several photographs of my mother when she was a girl. I was astonished. She was unimaginably gawky. My aunt says she had a lot of 'work' done. I didn't ask for details. I've seen a yearbook photograph of my father, and he wasn't much to look at, either. Apparently he had a lot of 'work' done, too."

"If you want to see all his year book photos, I have them in my office. They are of importance in another area. The librarian had ordered a set of his year book photos for me; and the bookkeeper at Valmont called to tell her that an unknown woman ordered a set and would be picking them up today or Monday. I waited in the Valmont parking lot all afternoon, but she didn't show up. I'll go back Monday and wait. Any ideas?"

"There were many women in my father's life. The most likely person is Loreen. But why would she want them?"

"I had a strange thought about that. Since Hiram didn't shoot himself and we've ruled out Tim and Mr. Michelson - since you were the apparent target, Loreen is probably the shooter. She may not have intended to shoot him... or maybe she did... but the fact is that if he survives she will need him to alibi her and to say, for example, that it was an unknown - preferably masked - male intruder. He may not want to go along with this lie. She might then threaten to plaster every telephone pole in the county with his pictures and make him a laughingstock. Your dad is, after all, a vain man."

"He is that, and cruelly so. My brother looked like him." Heidi turned her face away.

"There is another more delicate matter. Apparently, your dad does not have health insurance. Loreen said that under the terms of her divorce, her husband was going to pay for her health insurance and the four kids, but that she understood that your dad was also covered, as a 'spouse.' He isn't. Loreen says she can't pay the hospital bills. She wants you to pay."

Heidi shook het head. "Does it ever end? It's always more of the same. They'll kill me or lock me up in an asylum for my money but while I'm alive I'm obliged to sign their checks. That ship has sailed. I won't pay. They have an impressive jewelry collection. What other financial problems are there?"

"There's Tim's wife and her dialysis treatment - if she ever decides to take them. She felt so good after last week's treatment that she may agree to take more. Neither Tim nor his father has a medical plan. His dad qualifies for Medicare, but not Tim and certainly not his wife. I don't know if she is officially disabled or what. But she needs kidney treatments and if no one else pays for them, it is probably in your best interests to pay for them."

"Of course. I've been offering to do that for a long time. A kidney transplant, too."

"What if her recovery meant a restoration of her family?"

"You mean, if Tim went back to her?"

"Yes."

"I may be living in sin with him, but he was married in the Church. He's not divorced and if he wants to go back to her, either for her or for the kids, he'll go with my blessing. Certainly I will miss him. But maybe I'll get my teeth capped and some nose surgery. As my aunt would say, I'll get some work done. What do you think?"

"If you can afford it, get it. But don't agree to marry anyone until you've seen his prep school photos."

"Yes," Heidi agreed, "we don't want two dominant genes to meet up in a dark alley."

They laughed. Beryl said, "You seem knowledgeable about your legal position. I don't want to introduce an unpleasant topic, but I need to understand the flow of assets so that I can understand motives. If you die without a husband or children, your father inherits everything - assuming that you don't purposely exclude him. Is that right?"

"Yes. He's my only living relative."

"And if your father dies first, Loreen inherits nothing of yours."

"That's right. She is out of luck. She gets his personal assets and his liabilities. She can't touch anything of mine. Why do you ask?"

"Because I talked to Loreen and she seemed genuinely concerned about your father's survival... more concerned that I would have thought. She may be worried that he'll die before you."

"That must be a new kind of worry for her. But I still won't underwrite his medical bills. Let them spend their own money for a change."

FRIDAY, SATURDAY, SUNDAY, MONDAY, NOVEMBER 11, 12, 13, 14, 2011

For George, four days had compressed into glacial solidity. They were one event that was moving so imperceptibly that he could not detect any changes. He began to take an interest in the towns he passed. He'd exit the interstate and drive through a community and wish that he had a camera or knew more about painting or photography to record some of the interesting features of 'village life.' He was somebody else as he drove through these towns and he began to enjoy being this new person.

The vague desire to memorialize the people and landscapes he had seen became clearer and more substantive as he drove through the Painted Desert and the Petrified Forest. He seriously considered what it would take to become a competent photographer. He recalled the various photographers he had seen at crime scenes and at celebrity events. He could afford to be selective... artistic. He didn't want to photograph victims or join the ranks of the paparazzi. He decided this on Monday night as he stayed at a motel in Flagstaff, Arizona.

Someone once told him that inside every hard assed cop there lived a flower child. He wondered if perhaps there was an esthete inside him that had just awakened from a forty-three "or so" year nap.

For Beryl, the days passed in a hectic blur. All of the telephone calls that came in to the temple were forwarded to her. Early every morning, she had to dress and go to the temple to open the doors and then sit there, leading the little congregation in various chants and meditations, until the morning session was over. She would stand at the door, as Sensei always did, and say goodbye to each person who had attended. Then she would lock the temple and return to her own office to answer all the messages that had been left for her.

She had waited outside Valmont Prep and sure enough, Loreen came to purchase the photographs of her husband in his boyhood years. Beryl could imagine Loreen nailing copies of them to every telephone pole in the county. Hiram Bielmann's condition remained stubbornly static. Loreen's hopes were still alive.

The Bielmann case was not the only case she and George were working on. They had two cases that were waiting for an analysis of financial data to be completed and one case that was waiting for the surveillance progress reports of a foreign operative to be certifiably translated. Other cases were still in the discussion phase. All of them entailed a significant amount of communication, which meant hours spent talking on the phone or writing emails.

As far as Beryl's current situation was concerned, the Bielmann case required the most time consuming work of all: making unilateral decisions where collaborative decisions were needed.

George was always so dependable. Beryl understood the pain he felt. She wondered if he understood the burden his abrupt departure had placed upon her.

TUESDAY, NOVEMBER 15, 2011

George awakened Tuesday morning with a desire to see water. If he kept on going, Kingman would be the last Arizona city on his unscheduled itinerary. It was a decidedly boring town, he thought. He decided to take a side trip to Lake Havasu City to see London Bridge. Going south, he headed for the blue sky and water of one of the Colorado River's many lakes.

In a few hours he found himself leaning on the railing of the old stone bridge to watch the furrowed wakes of water skiers and the parasailers lifted high over the water by their colorful chutes. Imagine, he thought, it's November and there are still people playing in the water. Since he had no destination, he had no schedule; and freedom of this rarity had to be honored. He checked into a motel.

Fish and chips were not on his Philadelphia diet, but he was outside the jurisdiction of the diet police. He bought a six pack of beer, several orders of fish and chips 'to go,' and sat on the lawn outside his room, enjoying the sun and the antics of the small rabbits that darted across the grass. He felt different, sitting there. "I am transmorgrifying" he said using that odd-ball word that seemed now to express precisely how he felt. He was seeing things he had previously missed. These were new eyes that were opening a new mind. He watched the sun begin to drown in the horizon and the air take on the Purkinje effect's pinkish hue. Twenty years before, in Japan, he had seen Mount Fuji glow red early one morning. Photographers scrambled to capture the sight. He understood why they would want to memorialize beauty. With a picture, the world could see the mountain blush. One side of Havasu was in Arizona, but the other side was in California - and if a man wanted to delve into the photographic arts, this was the place to do it.

He spent a restful night.

WEDNESDAY, NOVEMBER 16, 2011

Before lunch, he checked out of the motel and got on the road again, heading for Barstow.

On the way he decided that the things he had seen were so absolutely fascinating that they should be locked in time like those people who were eternally posed 'on a grecian urn.' When he exited the interstate in Barstow, he stopped at a gas station and asked for directions to the best electronics store in town.

He bought a digital camera and a photography manual. "I want to see my photos on a screen," he said to the clerk who immediately guided him through the purchase of a computer. George's new person appeared to be as finicky as Goldilocks. The iPad was too small, and the desktop was too large. Finally he settled on the "just right" MacPro. The clerk offered to show him how to put his email address into it. George's new person responded with unaccustomed anger. "No! None of that online crap! I just want to look at the pictures I take!" He was assured that he did not have to share his photographs with anyone, not even his own personal email account.

The new person ran up his credit cards, but he did not care. He checked into a motel and read the photography text.

THURSDAY, NOVEMBER 17, 2011

George spent the morning in his new 'photog' persona, practicing on churches. He had lunch and took pictures of churches. He then decided that he would spend an additional night in Barstow in case he had to return to the store for further instructions. He was learning a lot about light, he told himself.

In his previous conversations with Beryl, nothing had happened that surprised him. Hiram had at first 'held his own' and, however pleasant this news must have seemed to Hiram's loved ones, his chance of surviving with a .38 slug in his head was, in George's opinion, less than zero.

He thought about Hiram's yearbook photographs. They demonstrated, in their own way, the significance of the art form.

There was little point in calling his office. He was a professional and, in his expert opinion, Loreen was the shooter. Once that had been determined, only a 'mop-up' gathering of evidence remained to be done.

By Thursday afternoon, he had exhausted Barstow's supply of churches. He got a kick out of the kids who thought he must be a professional photographer. He violated the rigorous exclusivity of his specialty and took photos of the kids.

By Thursday evening he was an adept in the loading of pictures into computers and viewing them on the screen. He began to perform with ease other alien electronic acts that had always confounded him. He recalled how the old George had felt more powerful than a Spartan Hoplite when he mastered programming his VCR. He still had not figured out his DVR, but now, he no longer cared to record 'other people's' art.

His life was flowing by in a gentle current that did not want to be impeded. "You cannot step into the same river twice," Sensei Percy Wong had said. George understood this fully.

FRIDAY, NOVEMBER 18, 2011

It occurred to him on Friday morning that he ought to call his ex-wife in Mendocino and talk to his kids. But he did not want to do this from a motel. He therefore got five dollars in quarters and found an old pay phone at a gas station. If they didn't feel like talking, he would have all those background noises to support his claim that his call was obviously intended to be brief. A servant answered and said the family was away on vacation. He said he'd call again in a month or so and hung up.

He returned to his room and called Beryl. "How is everyone?" he asked.

Beryl deliberately tried to relieve him of guilt. "Maybe you're a catalyst," she said. "While you're away, nothing seems to happen. The hacker has pulled CSI's sales slip for their Bielmann installation. Loreen ordered the system. He's yet to mine the records for a video record of the shooting. Heidi is fine but a little annoyed that her new brace hasn't arrived yet. The odds on Hiram's survival are beginning to shift against him. Everett Smith said that Sensei says that Lily 'kicks his ass' at chess."

"That's nice," the new person said. "It's good that they're getting along."

The motel had a laundromat and since he had all those quarters, he took all the clothing he had purchased at truck stops, and laundered them.

Wearing only a T-shirt and jeans, he drove to Newberry Springs to photograph interesting things at the nearby wilderness area. He got good shots of beckoning joshua trees, some yucca, and even a slightly out of place saguaro. The desert spoke to him, he decided, but the desert air did seem to tire him. Sometimes, he told himself, a man can get too much sunshine and fresh air. He felt his face and could tell that the sun had 'kissed' him. Yes, he'd look good with a little tan. He went back to the motel early and watched television.

Maybe he would stop to see the Salton Sea on his way back, if, in fact, he decided to go back via the southern route.

He spent his last night in Barstow.

SATURDAY, NOVEMBER 19, 2011

It was time to move on. The new person sought more interesting religious buildings... like old Spanish missions. He had photographed enough ordinary churches and mountains and sand. There were a few exceptional desert flowers in his collection; but it was time to move on.

He packed his things and locked them in his pickup. The day was clear... a good day to take photographs in San Diego.

He walked down to the desk and told them to prepare his bill. A mini-breakfast was provided in the office, and he stayed to have a cup of coffee and two donuts. As he signed the credit card invoice, the clerk asked, "You headed for the San Berdu?"

"What?" said the new person.

"The San Berdu Freeway. *San Bernadino.*"

George pushed the new person out of the way. "San Bernadino? No. What the hell would I be doing in San Bernadino?"

"Sorry, Mister," said the clerk. "I didn't mean to offen'ja."

George drove his pickup to the Interstate and headed east. He made only brief stops, and seventeen hours later he checked into a motel in Amarillo, Texas.

SUNDAY, NOVEMBER 20, 2011

George got up too early to call Beryl. He stopped for breakfast at a truck stop diner and was back on the Interstate by dawn.

He drove relentlessly, and crossed the Mississippi at Saint Louis, Missouri, continuing on until fatigue overtook his ambition. He stopped in Indianapolis and collapsed on the bed of a motel.

MONDAY, NOVEMBER 21, 2011

At dawn he called Beryl. "What's new with the case," he asked.

"Jeff Gable's anonymous man hacked into CSI's files and will try to meet us to review the entire video record. We hope to get it tomorrow." She did not tell him that she asked the hacker to review the hours of action and to select segments that he thought were worthy of notice. She was so busy with the temple and the office that she had no time to do any constructive work on the case.

"Loreen is the shooter," George quietly announced. "So, how are the sick people and the pretending to be sick people?"

"They are concerned about Hiram. He's still in the ICU. Heidi got her corset, but because of the security problem, she's been happy to stay in the hospital. This separation from Tim seems to have given each of them time to think. Tim's wife has agreed to have dialysis treatments. She's also agreeable to getting a kidney transplant. She's on an organ waiting list."

"If Tim's wife can start living a normal life, maybe he'll go back to her. How is Heidi taking that possibility?"

"Extremely well. She doesn't want to lose him but realizes that he is committed elsewhere. He says they're both Catholics of convenience. 'Form precedes function,' he told me. And speaking of form, Heidi's thinking about getting her own plastic surgery done... nose... teeth. She's also done a lot of thinking about her father's actions. His treatment of her brother and the way he tried to hire us in an attempt to have her declared mentally incompetent. She's taking a hard line. Good for her. So, where are you?" Beryl asked.

"I think I'm in Indianapolis. No," he looked at some brochures on his bedside table, "I'm sure I'm in Indianapolis. I'll be home in another twelve hours, I guess. I'll come right to the office. You can try to cook dinner for me."

"I can try to make you your favorite TV dinners. Name your poison. No raw vegetables for one time only."

"Get me a couple of those spaghetti and meat sauce things with mushrooms, for people on a diet. Get me maybe three of them. And some of that carrot cake I like."

"Yes, Master."

George hung up. Beryl had to steady herself to keep from crying. George was back on the job.

At nine o'clock George parked his pickup in the rear of the office, and with unusual quickness climbed the stairs to Beryl's second floor apartment. The light was on in the kitchen. He knocked once and she came out of her bedroom/office to open the door.

"Welcome aboard," she said.

George put his arms around her and squeezed her tightly. "I'm starved. Don't tell me how you've been slaving over a hot microwave... just get me that spaghetti stuff I like."

"Go wash your hands. God knows what you've been touching for the last thousand miles."

"Seven hundred," he yelled in correction as he went into the bathroom.

TUESDAY, NOVEMBER 22, 2011

George had been reunited with his medications late Monday night. After wolfing down three TV dinners and several pieces of cake, the digestion of which required a considerable amount of blood to be diverted to his abdomen, his nervous system quickly showed the strain of prolonged tension. Tired but not calm, he could barely finish the drive home to his house. His bed was a welcomed sight and he dropped on it expecting to fall asleep instantly. His nerves, however, sizzled like lit fuses, and after a few minutes of trying and failing to relax, he bolted into the bathroom and took his arthritis and pain pills. He slept in total oblivion and was still groggy when Beryl arrived at eleven o'clock.

She had knocked repeatedly and, after getting no response, had let herself in. She shook him and shouted until he awakened. He sat up, rubbed his eyes, mumbled something and went into the bathroom to shower. Beryl put the kettle on and defrosted some pastries.

"What's so urgent?" he asked when he finally sat across the table from her.

"I talked to Jeff Gable earlier. His anonymous hacker friend was able to access the video files and retrieve all the recordings that the CSI company made. Hacking into their system wasn't cheap and naturally, we're not allowed to tell anyone we ordered the work. Anyway, he's finished, and we've got an appointment with him at one o'clock."

George was still groggy and cranky. "Why does he have to present the recordings to us? Why can't he just turn them over? This isn't professional."

Beryl's expression hardened into one that conveyed the news that the 'line of tolerance' had just been crossed. "I'm going to pretend that I didn't hear what you just said. As far as he's concerned, they're contraband. Drink your bloody tea and get your jacket. We're late. I also talked to Everett Smith and told him we'd stop by Tarleton to touch base with him. He and Sanford were on their way down from Jim Thorpe on their daily food run. We should have arrived at the same time. As it is, we'll be lucky to catch them before they head back." She stood up, pushed her chair back against the table, and headed for the door.

George gathered the dishes and put them in the sink. He noticed that his house plants were in perfect condition. "Thanks for keeping the plants watered," he called as he followed her out of the house.

"I've lost a whole size," Everett Smith confided as they sat in his study, waiting for the cook to finish preparing the 'food to go.' "My waist is now what it was when I was in college."

"I've been run ragged, too," Beryl commiserated. "Since the night Heidi was injured, I've been alone in the office, and then when Sensei went up to the cabin, I've had to open and close the temple and stay for the duration of the services. All the calls are forwarded to me. And I've kept the plants watered in Sensei's apartment, in the temple, at George's house, my apartment, and the office. It's been frenetic. I've been visiting patients in hospitals and for two days had to stake out a prep school - all while conducting an investigation."

"No help from George?" Everett asked.

George lowered his gaze and said simply, "I was away."

"Lily's been asking for you. She thinks you're deliberately avoiding her."

George grunted. "I was in Southern California. I took a lot of pictures. I'll show them to her when she gets back."

Cecelia Smith held up a newspaper. "Did you see the morning papers?" she asked.

"No," Beryl said. "What did we miss?"

"Well," Cecelia replied, "some reporter with a telephoto lens got a picture of Lily posing as Heidi, standing outside the cabin door, and walking on her own. The story posed the question, 'Miracle at Jim Thorpe?' It seems that Swami George has quite a healing touch."

"Yes," said Beryl. "When it comes to the 'Laying on of hands,' he has no equal."

George nudged her. "I'm glad this nightmare is almost over. Isn't Heidi supposed to be released soon? Has there been any change in that?"

"No," replied Cecelia. "I said that she should be brought here to recuperate, but under whose name, I do not know. This has been so confusing. I don't think the police have a clue about what happened out at Black Walnut."

Everett summed up the case as he understood it. "Hiram is getting worse. Ainsley Fallon called me to say, in that staccato way he has of speaking medibabble, 'TBI Traumatic Brain Injury... cascading effects... respiratory complications... heavy smoking did not help... craniotomy relieved pressure... vital signs not good.' Or, something like that.

"The police are stymied in their search for a pair of would-be killers. They have tried to mix and match all the separates. Tim and Loreen. Tim and his father. His father and Loreen. One of Loreen's relatives and Loreen. Tim's wife and Tim. Tim's wife and his father. To my knowledge they have not tried Tim's wife and Loreen... but no doubt they are considering that, even as we speak.

"Tim's wife had a reprieve. After neighbors took advantage of a near death crisis to get her on dialysis, although she fought it, she felt so good that she went shopping. Naturally, the police figure that if she was strong enough to go to the market, she was capable of driving out to the estate, connecting with her partner in crime, shooting Hiram, and pushing Heidi down the stairs."

George asked, "Why do they think there are two people... a pair of killers?"

"Heidi was convinced that the actions were simultaneous," Everett explained. "Everybody that possibly was involved is right handed. The gun had to be in the shooter's right hand, and her father was behind her on her left. The shooter would have to cross his arms to shoot and push at the same time."

"The reasoning is faulty," George replied. "People hear the word 'push' and think of a hand. When you restrict yourself to a familiar cause and effect order, you begin to skew the facts. Here's an example: "Let's say you have two boxes that are identical in size. One box is filled to the top with gold coins each of which is worth five hundred dollars. The other is filled to exactly the half way point with gold coins each of which is worth one thousand dollars. Which box is worth more?"

Everyone thought. Beryl said nothing. George's earlier criticism about the hacker had silenced her. She had had several long discussions with Jeff Gable regarding the images that the CSI files contained. She knew where the guilt lay just as she knew the solution to the gold coin problem.

Everett and Cecilia Smith and Sanford agreed that the two boxes were of equal value.

"Tell them," George said to Beryl.

"The box that has the five hundred dollar coins is worth more."

"Why?" asked Everett.

"Because," Beryl replied, "It is filled to the top with gold while the other box is only half filled."

"Oh, Jesus!" Everett shouted, "And big coins cannot be as efficiently packaged as small ones."

George had finally awakened. "Beryl said that Heidi insisted that there were two separate actions: her father got shot and she got pushed. She also said that her father had tilted the wheelchair onto its left wheel and maybe was reaching for the right wheel to rotate the chair. He was hit in the right forehead so we can suppose that he had looked around and was maybe slightly bent over. The shot knocked him against the wheelchair and down they both went. One shot. One continuous action... shot, shove, fall."

Beryl clarified motives. "Tim has no motive to kill Hiram or Heidi. Zero motive. And neither do Tim's wife and his father... absolutely no motive to destroy and a definite motive to preserve. The kids were at school. This was verified. That leaves Loreen."

Jeff Gable began the presentation. "We copied the entire Bielmann file, which includes the invoice and the document that falsely grants them permission to install the surveillance equipment. As to the surveillance, itself," Jeff directed his comments to George, "none of our equipment was in place. CSI's images are sub-standard but revealing, nevertheless. We've culled the scenes for possible relevance and made a selection which I've already discussed with Beryl.

"They had two cameras in the hallway. I should add that in my personal opinion, Hiram Bielmann did not know that this surveillance was ongoing. In several scenes he's picking his nose. In my experience, a person who knows he's on camera doesn't scratch his testicles or pick his nose or do anything that he wouldn't want memorialized. On the other hand, Heidi is caught walking in one opening sequence. I'll let Beryl supply the voice-over."

Beryl began by giving a preface to the image on screen. "This is my theory of the crime. Heidi had a heart-to-heart talk with her broker. Evidently, Hiram preferred to determine for himself which stocks he would invest in. He repeatedly blundered. A Ponzi scheme had cost him more than a million. Not only had Hiram spent all his money, he now owed quite a few people considerable sums. Loreen has been under enormous stress for so long that her sanity is beginning to crack.

"For her, this year was particularly devastating. Hiram's claim that the divorce documents were signed under duress isn't getting anywhere. She knows their only chance to get control of all that money is to have Heidi declared dead or mentally incompetent. Obviously, the declaration has a condition. Heidi must be single. If she marries Tim, he will see to it that he inherits everything. If she dies while she is single, Hiram is her only living heir. And naturally, if she marries, her father will have no standing when it comes to having her declared mentally incompetent.

"Loreen's only connection to the money is as Hiram's wife. Her attempts to get pregnant have failed just as her attempts to have her children legally adopted have failed. Hiram is a known philanderer. She may fear - not without reason - that Hiram may be using her and her kids' presence at Black Walnut Farm to bolster his claim to the estate. He can be seen as a responsible 'head of family.' If he can't succeed in getting

Heidi declared incompetent, he may not want to be saddled with Loreen and *her* four kids, and then he'll dump her. She'll get nothing.

"To Loreen, it becomes imperative to end Heidi's life, and the sooner, the better. Fuzzy possibilities form in her mind. She and Hiram see a lawyer. He recommends a P.I. She and Hiram see George on November 2nd and learn that installing surveillance equipment is going to be expensive. They're broke and proceed to do it on the cheap. One of the cameras catches Heidi walking around. Loreen knows she's sexually active with Tim and that she's not crippled. At first Loreen must think that this will support their claim that Heidi is mentally defective; but then she thinks, 'Ah, no one knows about the surveillance. If I say nothing I can claim that I believed she truly was crippled and then I can stage a home invasion and claim that I shot and killed an intruder who was *standing* in a doorway. Obviously I could not have expected a standing person to be Heidi. And then a subsequent investigation will reveal to my surprise that Heidi had been faking her injury.' It must seem perfect to Loreen.

"Hiram wants to proceed with establishing Heidi's mental incompetence. Loreen knows how this will drag on and on. She will pretend to be in accord with this strategy. But she will not wait to act. She cannot afford to wait. She knows there's a gun in the attic."

Beryl looked at the screen. "Here she is on November 4th, Friday morning." Gable let the video roll. "She walks down the hall and opens a door that leads to a stairway to the third floor. The servants' rooms are in one wing of the third floor and some guest rooms are in the other. We also know that there is a pull-down ladder in the ceiling of the third floor - a ladder that goes up to the attic. Note that she is wearing a clean dark sweater and her hair is precisely combed. She'll be up there for two hours, and in the interim only the chambermaid appears in the footage.

"Here she is after those two hours. Look at her! She's a mess!" Beryl turned to Jeff Gable. "It's just as you described it!" She resumed her narrative. "The shoulders of the dark sweater are covered with dust. No doubt when she pulled down the ladder or rifled through the attic files, she got showered with it. Her hair looks like she tried to pull it out. It's wild. And she has been crying. Look at her face." He froze the picture to show Loreen's tear-streaked face and a clearly frantic expression. And what is Loreen carrying? Ah, that metal object looks like a revolver to me. An old sixgun that she's holding by the barrel." Gable enlarged the gun.

George sat up. "It looks like a Colt .38 *Police Positive*. A famous gun. I can recognize it from here."

Beryl continued, "That's what it is - a Colt .38. Heidi told me yesterday. After I talked to Jeff, I asked her what else was up there. She said, 'income tax and other personal records, school papers and yearbooks, fraternity stuff, old sports' equipment, and odds and ends.' I asked Heidi to have Mr. Michelson find out what Loreen was looking at. He looked and said that old medical records were scattered all over the floor. Heidi couldn't tell him where she was, but she told him to give me the records if I came by and asked for them. It's worth noting that Hiram's prep school year books are up there and if Loreen got a look at the "before" pictures of Hiram - that's before cosmetic surgery - she might see an opportunity for 'leverage.' We know that she will soon order a set of yearbook photos. Hiram is a conceited fellow. Maybe she intends to blackmail him with the photos if he doesn't go along with her scheme and alibi her, or if he thinks about dumping her. No matter. She went up for the gun and she came down with it."

"What else is interesting in the video record?" George asked.

"I'll jump to the shooting," Jeff said. "Here is Tuesday, November 8th."

"Here we are," Beryl said, "it's 16:40. Loreen has probably heard that Tim's wife wanted the children to stay for a few extra hours. Loreen may think that his wife is close to death. Time is running out for Loreen. There will never be another day as perfect for a version of the "intruder" killing as Election Day when everyone is out of the house. Yes, she can claim that Heidi was shot by an intruder. The gun is old and hasn't been used in a generation. She can simply get rid of it and dare Hiram to try to contradict her. Quite possibly she has not put fresh ammo into the gun and the pistol's firing power isn't what it should be. Normally, we'd expect the .38 to go through his skull. But, I digress.

"Hiram is wheeling Heidi out of her bedroom. We switch cameras. They continue on towards the top of the stairs. On the right side, behind them, coming out of a bedroom is Loreen, gun in hand. Hiram stops the old stiff wheelchair near the top of the stairs. He tilts it slightly on its left wheel and then bends over a little to grab the wheel to turn it, looks up, and says something. Loreen's body then blocks most of the action. She apparently fires since Hiram and Heidi fall out of the picture. Loreen descends the stairs but not far enough to get out of the picture. We can still see the top of her head so we know she went down to just about where Hiram was found. I guess she sees that he's alive. Now look! Her head turns and looks down into the foyer towards the front door. This is just about the time that Tim says the kids entered the house after he parked the car. Loreen rushes up the stairs! Look at the expression on her face! She's crazed. She's mumbling something as she runs. She passes under the camera. The other camera picks her up. The only thing back there is a servant's staircase that goes to the kitchen. She has to get out of the house if she's ever going to blame Tim or his father or anybody else. We know that Tim will find her back in the carriage house ten minutes or so later."

Beryl took the office checkbook out of her tote bag. "Nice job, Jeffrey. What do you want to call this?"

"Make it a consultation fee. Don't put the Black Walnut reference on the check," Gable advised.

As Beryl wrote out the check she said, "Hang onto the complete file, but give me a copy of those selections."

"I've already made one." Gable exchanged the copy for the check.

Their next stop was Black Walnut Farm. Beryl made sure that neither the Mercedes nor the Escalade was in the parking area.

Tim's father answered the door, carrying a stack of papers. "I saw you come up the driveway," he said, "and knew what you were here for." He handed the papers to Beryl. "These are just the medical records. Good luck with finding whatever it was Loreen found. I think you'll find it on top of the pile."

Beryl thanked him and gave the stack to George.

As they drove back to the office, George examined the documents, starting with the top one. "Jesus," he said quietly. "It's a urologist's bill for a vasectomy Hiram had back in 2001."

Beryl whooped. "What?" She whooped again. "And I thought she was aiming for Heidi and shot him by accident. She was probably mad enough to shoot him."

George recalled her story about trying to get pregnant. "She followed all that pregnancy kit stuff. Four years of monitoring herself to find out when she was ovulating."

"No wonder she was crazed. It was a 'devil may care' recklessness. No real planning. Just wild craziness." Beryl laughed. "That's enough to make any woman a homicidal maniac."

George closed the files. "Whoa!" he shouted. "Lily! That good PR newspaper photo Cecelia Smith saw this morning is now a threat. Loreen is armed and she's desperate. If Hiram's condition worsened, she will need to get rid of Heidi if she's got any chance left to get the money. That puts Lily in danger. Let's get moving! Are you carrying?"

Beryl's eyes widened. She understood the urgency. "No. Your Smith & Wesson .38 is in the glove compartment. I use it for practice at the range. Can you handle it?"

"I haven't fired a revolver in years. I got used to the semi. We'd lose too much time if we detour back to my house or the office. I'll make it work."

"Let's swing by Memorial hospital since it's on our way to the highway north. If Loreen's car is there, we won't need to rush. Take my phone and get Dr. Fallon on the line. He needs to order extra security put on Heidi's room at Saint Luke's just in case Loreen finds out where Heidi really is."

Dr. Fallon understood perfectly. When George told him that Heidi needed guards immediately, he said, simply, "Twenty-four, seven. Got it."

They circled the hospital twice. Loreen's Mercedes was nowhere in sight. They headed for the mountains.

Loreen Bielmann, dressed in dark clothing, her face nearly obscured by the fur trimmed hood of the parka she wore, followed a map she had printed from an internet search. Intending to approach the cabin from the rear, she parked in a leveled area two miles away. What had appeared flat on the map, was actually a tree filled, rocky hillside. She carried the .38 Colt 'Police Positive' revolver, a hunting knife, and a Remington .32 rifle with a gunsight that the salesman helped her to "zero in" for her specific use. He suggested that she purchase a shoulder sling for the weapon, but she declined, thinking it unnecessary. Aside from misperceiving the lay of the land from the flat map, she underestimated the increased difficulty that hand-carrying a rifle would cause.

The approaching winter solstice made the day shorter than she had expected. Still, there was plenty of daylight left as she reached the back side base of the hill on which Sensei's cabin stood. A creek had eroded the topsoil and carved a ditch that blocked her path; and she saw that she would have to wade across the water if she intended to climb the hill and reach any location from which she could shoot. She began to scale the steep hillside but half-way up she encountered so many rocky outcrops that, with one hand needed to hold the rifle, she could not continue to climb. She returned to the creek and followed it back in the direction of the area in which the map indicated the van should be parked.

She had not known that when Sanford and Everett Smith delivered food to the cabin they would immediately bring down a tray of dirty dishes, laundry, a laptop, and anything else they intended to take back to Tarleton House. This ensured that they could stay at the cabin and visit for a few hours without having to worry about carrying such items down the slippery path in rain or approaching darkness. Loreen walked up to the van and looked in the passenger-side window. She could see the basket of dirty dishes on the floor just behind the front seats. The van was not locked. She slid the door open, picked up a dish, and, with the aid of a small penlight, examined the hallmark. She read "Haviland" and decided that the dish had probably come from her own cupboard. "While you were at the hospital," she whispered to herself, "Tim no doubt helped himself to whatever he wanted just to bring food to his 'meal-ticket' Heidi." She cursed him and slammed the door shut.

"What about that faith healer?" she asked herself. He was not the detective she hired. "He had to be another one of the quacks. The smart thing would be to shoot him. There would be one less irritant in the world." She believed that Heidi was no more injured now than she had been before. "The cozy little cabin," she whispered, "Heidi's Blue Heaven." She wondered if Tim drove the faith healer down to the motel lodge at sundown so that he and Heidi could be alone to make plans and a baby. This thought antagonized her into an even more irrational state. She suddenly drew the revolver and shot the van's front tires, thinking that when Tim came to investigate the shots, she'd shoot him, too. With Tim dead, Heidi would be vulnerable. "You'd have to shoot them all," she informed herself. "You can't leave any witnesses." This seemed to be both logical and foolproof.

At the sound of the shots, the cabin door opened and the interior light illuminated several men who came out to investigate. Loreen had clearly seen the men in the doorway, and neither one was Tim. She didn't know who they were and for a moment she wondered if she had the correct cabin. But the Haviland porcelain dish convinced her that she was correct. Whoever they were, they were witnesses. She aimed her rifle and fired at them. The shots missed, but both Sanford and Everett Smith dove down for cover and slid some thirty feet down the loose rocks that were above the boulders that originally had blocked Loreen's way. Both men grunted and yelped as they lost their footing and slid. Loreen smiled. If they were merely injured, she would go and finish them off. She began to creep up the slope.

Sensei had immediately extinguished the lamps, but he had no water within reach to douse the fire in the little iron stove. He immediately attended to Lily. He looked for her cap and wig. The top burner hole was uncovered and the firelight glowed gold and orange in the darkened room. "Find your Kevlar cap and get under the blanket!"

The moon was nearly full and its light was sufficient for someone to follow the path up to the cabin. Sensei pushed Lilyanne under the blanket and waited.

At sundown, Beryl and George had gotten onto the Interstate and hooked onto the road which took them past the lodge in Jim Thorpe where Everett Smith and Sanford were staying. They proceeded to Route 209 which delivered them to the dirt road that went to the cabin's parking area. As they neared the area they heard two shots, and then a minute later, two more shots. "She's definitely here," Beryl said.

The van was in the parking lot, its punctured front tires flat on the ground. Everett and Sanford were not around. In the event they were hiding nearby, Beryl called softly, "Mr. Smith! Sanford! It's Beryl and George." There was no answer.

Loreen reached the flagstone deck in front of the cabin as Beryl and George began to climb the slope. She could clearly see an aluminum chaise longue propped up against the cabin near the front door. She picked up several rocks and went as far to the side of the cabin as she could while still being able to throw the rocks at the door. The first rock landed near the door. Lily exclaimed, "Maybe it's my father. Maybe he's hurt. You have to look!" Sensei did not want to open the door. Lily pleaded, "Please. Maybe it's my father or Sanford!"

Loreen could hear a female voice but she could not determine what the voice was saying. She moved closer to the front and threw another rock. This time the rock struck the door. Lily cried out, "Please!"

Sensei relented. "Stay down," he said.

Loreen stood behind the chaise longue and waited. Sensei opened the front door and stepped out onto the flagstone deck. "Mr. Smith!" he called. With one great push, Loreen forced the chaise longue against him, knocking him down under a tangle of aluminum bars and foam padding. She leaped onto the threshold, entered the cabin, and tried to grab Lily by the hair with her left hand. Startled by the cap and wig that came off in her hand, she swung the rifle at Lily, hitting her in the face. Lily staggered as Loreen dropped the rifle and wig, and reached for her hair again as she pulled the hunting knife from its sheath. With Lily's hair firmly in her grasp, Loreen held the blade to her throat. Sensei stood in the doorway and stopped moving. In the stove's light, he could see the knife's point suddenly make a dimple in Lily's throat. "Don't hurt her!" he pleaded. "Take whatever you want, but don't hurt her."

Loreen screamed, "Where is she? Where is Heidi?"

George and Beryl were now some thirty feet from the top of the hill. They could hear Sensei beg, "Stay calm. Please just calm down. I'll take you to Heidi. Just stay calm."

They continued to scramble up the hill until they could see Sensei and a sliver of light between him and the door jamb. "Wait here," George whispered, "while I find a better position. Percy's blocking my shot." He moved ten feet to his left. "I can just about see Lily and the glint of a blade. Christ! She's got a knife to her throat. I can't get a shot off! Sensei's in my line of fire."

George could not get a better angle. The sliver of light between Sensei's body and the door jamb gave him the only view of the interior. He heard Loreen continue to shout, "Where is she?" Then she snarled, "What the hell is going on here? Where is Heidi?" She tightened her grip on Lily's hair and pushed the tip of the blade far enough into the skin to cause a trickle of blood to run down into her blouse.

Through the ribbon of light, George could clearly see the figure with the parka, the shiny blade at Lily's throat, and the trickle of blood.

George Wagner would later say that what he did next was stupid, unworthy of a rational human being, and certainly outrageous for any person who respected the law and human life to do. He drew his Smith and Wesson, put it in his weakened right hand, aimed it and put his left index finger over his right index finger and squeezed the trigger, sending a bullet through the narrow opening directly into Loreen's forehead. Lily stood frozen and speechless as Loreen's head snapped back and she dropped to the cabin floor. Sensei rushed in and grabbed Lily. Holding her, he went to the doorway and cried, "Mr. Smith. Sanford! Lily's fine!" The two men came out from where they were hiding. "Put some more light on," Sanford shouted, and Sensei struck a match and lit the lamp.

George did not attempt to enter the cabin. Instead he grabbed Beryl's arm. "Let's just go back. I don't want any of that blubbering on me again."

"Go back where?"

"Home. Let's just go back home!"

"What is wrong with you? The van's been shot up. How do you expect them to get back? Flap their wings?" She climbed onto the cabin's front deck and rushed into the hectic scene. "Any leftovers?" she asked. "I'm starving."

The Carbon County Police Department came to the site and Everett Smith, using all the connections he had in the Commonwealth, obtained permission for everyone, "in my party" to leave. "I have had all the trouble I care to have in Penn's Woods," he said.

Beryl drove and George, given his bad leg and arm, was given the more comfortable passenger's seat. Lilyanne, she said, should sit on George's lap where she was determined to sit anyway. That let Sensei, Smith and Sanford, the three faith healing clerics from points unknown, sit in the back seat of the Bronco.

George, embarrassed to have Lily perched on his lap, stared out the side window. Lilyanne, as expected, called him her "Crack shot Beast" and smothered his face in little kisses as she mussed his hair. George did not overtly respond to any of the petting.

Sensei tried to relieve the awkward situation by making small talk. "Dude!" he said to George, "That was one hell of a shot you took." George grunted.

"Modesty!" said Beryl. "It is his greatest virtue."

"I'm not being modest," George finally said. "I'm still stunned to think that I risked taking the shot. I'm not the marksman I used to be."

As they neared the city, Lily, subdued from fear and relief, begged George, Sensei and Beryl to come to Tarleton House for dinner. George declined and the others followed. "It's late," Beryl said, "and we're all exhausted."

It was after midnight when Beryl and two of the faith-healers pulled into the parking space behind the office. Everyone got out of the Bronco.

Sensei was already excited about his Thanksgiving Day date with the fabulous Miss Sonya Lee. He chattered on, "I'm wearing an heirloom Tang suit... incredible silk. Red. Miss Lee loves red." He turned to Beryl,

"My car's still at Tarleton. Will you take me to the airport tomorrow morning?"

"But of course," she replied.

"No!" George countered. "Let her sleep. Call me. I'll definitely keep my phone connected." Sensei agreed.

Beryl let Sensei out at the temple and then continued on to drop George off in front of his house.

As he entered his house, George realized that he had not checked to see if Beryl had watered the plants that he kept in an upstairs bedroom. This thought persisted and he immediately went upstairs and saw that Beryl had indeed watered the plants.

There was a large bathtub upstairs. He thought, "It's a great time to take a hot bath and get some of the dirt out of my fingernails." He looked at his pants, shoes and socks. "It's like being in a combat zone. Crawling in the muck."

He turned on the hot water and stripped. There was 'Jamaican Lime' body wash in the closet. He dumped half a bottle of it into the stream of water. He smiled, relaxed, and fell asleep leaning back in the comfortable tub. When the water grew cold, it awakened him and he went downstairs to bed.

WEDNESDAY, NOVEMBER 23, 2011

At 8 a.m. Sensei called. George was ready. He got into his pickup and set out to take Sensei to the airport to take the plane to San Diego. He thought it was particularly weird that he had been so close to San Diego only a few days before. "It is a small world," he philosophically noted.

On the way back from the airport he stopped at a bakery to buy some pastries for Beryl.

At ten o'clock he went to his office, checked the phone messages, and went upstairs to Beryl's apartment. To his surprise, she was up and dressed and about to leave to meet Alicia Eckersley who was in charge of the Thanksgiving Day meal that would be served the next day at a recently renovated hospice in Camden, New Jersey.

"Why don't you come along and help with the arrangements," Beryl asked. "God knows what Alicia has in mind. I've learned that it's best not to ask her for explanations about anything. Generate some good will. Help out at a hospice for the poor. It's Thanksgiving. Remember: "to protect and serve" and all that benevolent cop stuff."

George gave her his sideways look. "And I suppose Willem deVries is going to be there."

"You suppose correctly. He's the pastor. That is his ministry."

"You go ahead and do your good deed for the day. Will it be the whole day?"

"I don't think so. But with Alicia Eckersley one never knows."

"No, one doesn't."

"Help me load my car and stop feeling sorry for yourself." She stopped, suddenly remembering the temple. "Oh, Lord! Who will be watching the temple? I completely forgot to ask Sensei."

"I'll stay at the temple and keep the door mat out for the thundering herd. There are books to read and football games to watch. I'll think of something."

Lily called the office, but there was no answer. Beryl's cell went to voicemail. So did George's, although he had not taken his cellphone with him and did not know this.

At nine o'clock he closed the temple and walked down to the rear of the office to get his pickup truck. A light was on in Beryl's kitchen. He thought he'd go up and have some of those pastries and tea with her, but there in the kitchen light, Beryl was laughing with Willem deVries. George stood there stunned to see 'Father Bill' grab Beryl from behind, put his arms around her, and playfully bite her neck. She pushed him away, turned around, laughed, and he grabbed her again and this time he kissed her. George felt wounded and did not know why it should upset him. He knew many of the men who "waltzed" in and out of Beryl's life. Why DeVries? Why now? Why anything? Disgusted, he got into his pickup and began the drive home.

He turned on music and then decided that he didn't feel like listening to music. Sensei was probably with Miss Lee by now. "My life is shit," he said aloud, repeating the sentence as though it were a mantra. He pulled into his driveway and parked. For a few minutes he sat behind the wheel and stared at his front door. This time, he did not slump over the steering wheel and wonder about the quality of his life. "To hell with it," he announced, cutting off any possible dialogue with the steering wheel.

George poured orange juice into a glass and turned on the TV. His recliner was comfortable but he was too agitated to relax. He squirmed and shifted his weight. He decided that he didn't want to fall asleep in the chair. It would get cold and he wouldn't have a blanket and then he'd wake up and it would be dark and he would stumble trying to find the goddamned light and then he would get so agitated that he wouldn't be able to get to sleep and he'd wind up taking more of his goddamned pain medication than he needed and Christ knows he didn't want to get hooked on his lousy pain pills again. "Bullshit!" he said angrily. He turned off the TV. "Time for bed."

He picked up his prescription bottles, and in the chains of a blue funk that he could not consciously break, he opted for drugged freedom - and took one pill from each bottle.

Quickly, he stripped, got into his downstairs shower, washed his hair and blow dried it just in time to feel the medication kick in. Naked, he got into his kitchen-corner bed. In five minutes he was sound asleep.

Three hours passed. He did not see or hear a white Jaguar pull up beside his truck and park so cock-eyed that the chrysanthemums on the right side of the driveway were flattened. He did not hear the key to the panic room of Lily's heart insert itself into the front door. He did not hear her cross the tatami platforms that covered the floors of his new Japanese renovations. He did not see how she looked at his new decor with admiration and delight.

She saw him in the faint light that came in from the patio's lamp. She touched his unvarnished hair and stripped off her clothing and climbed into bed beside him. She kissed him lightly on his face and ears and neck. She caressed his body with her now-warm hands.

George murmured her name. He was, he truly believed, in the midst of a lovely wet dream. The weight of the girl pressed down on him as she straddled his body. He felt good. He felt very good. He put his hands on her arms and pulled her down onto him and felt her face rub against his. Immediately he woke up and pushed her back. "What the hell...! What the hell are you doing?"

Lilyanne leaned forward and again rubbed her face against his cheek. She whispered in his ear, "Shhhh... my sexy beast."

George groaned. "Oh, my God! Now what? Now what?" And then he began to kiss her the way he had always dreamed of kissing her.